D1034892

ROUGHSTOCK

Also by Laura Crum

Cutter
Hoofprints

ROUGHSTOCK

LAURA CRUM

ST. MARTIN'S PRESS ❧ NEW YORK

DEER PARK PUBLIC LIBRARY
44 LAKE AVENUE
DEER PARK, NY 11729

A THOMAS DUNNE BOOK.
An imprint of St. Martin's Press.

ROUGHSTOCK. Copyright © 1997 by Laura Crum. All rights reserved. Printed
in the United States of America. No part of this book may be used or
reproduced in any manner whatsoever without written permission except in
the case of brief quotations embodied in critical articles or reviews. For
information, address St. Martin's Press, 175 Fifth Avenue, New York, N.Y.
10010.

Library of Congress Cataloging-in-Publication Data

Crum, Laura.
    Roughstock / Laura Crum.
        p. cm.
    "A Thomas Dunne Book."
    ISBN 0-312-15643-X
    1. Women veterinarians—in California—Fiction.   2. Santa Cruz
(Calif.)—Fiction.   I. Title.
    PS3553.R76R68   1997
    813'.54—dc21   97-1831
                                                                       CIP

First Edition: August 1997

10 9 8 7 6 5 4 3 2 1

For Bill, with love, always.

With thanks to my mother, Joan Awbrey Brown, who bought ET, and my father, Barclay Kirk Brown, who helped buy Freddy— strictly out of the goodness of their hearts and despite a distinct lack of interest in horses.

Thanks also to Sue Crocker, Wally Evans, Brian Peters, and Craig Evans, DVM, the friends who have helped me with my horses for many years and provided much of the inspiration for these stories.

I would also like to thank everyone at Adobe Animal Hospital, my real-life veterinarians, who put up with my questions more or less patiently (especially Craig), and Lieutenant Patty Sapone of the Santa Cruz Police Department, who advises me on cops and their ways. All mistakes are mine, and probably arise from not asking enough questions.

Finally, I'd like to thank all the ropers, cutters, horse trainers, ranchers, packers, and working cowboys with whom I've spent many happy hours on horseback. These books could never have been written without you.

AUTHOR'S NOTE

All the human characters in this book are completely imaginary and are meant to resemble no one, living or dead.

Both Santa Cruz County and Lake Tahoe are real places, but they have been altered significantly to fit the purposes of the story. Imaginary towns, ranches, restaurants, casinos, streets, parks . . . etc. have been created where none exist, and the reader should not imagine that any of these places resemble the real casinos, ranches . . . etc. that do exist and might not be flattered by the comparison.

ROUGHSTOCK

ONE

I threw my clothes bag down on the elegantly carpeted floor of the Foresta Hotel in Northshore Village, Nevada, and stared out the window at the gray-blue expanse of Lake Tahoe. White-frosted pine trees and a backdrop of snowy peaks made the view even more spectacular than usual. I was here, at last, on my first vacation since I'd gone to work as a veterinarian, two and a half years earlier.

Well, almost a vacation. I was actually attending the annual Winter Equine Seminar, a three-day session of lectures on horse health problems. The interesting thing about the seminar was that classes were held from seven to ten in the morning and from four until seven in the evening. This left the middle of the day free for skiing, which was the point, more or less.

Skiing. I hadn't been skiing for three years. Nor had I been up here in the Sierra Nevada Mountains—to my way of thinking the most beautiful place on earth. Saying I was thrilled would be putting it mildly.

Blue stretched stiffly on the floor next to me and wagged his stump of a tail to get my attention. I reached down and rubbed his ears, not taking my eyes off the view. I'd smuggled the old dog in moments ago in an extralarge duffel bag I kept for the purpose. He knew the routine; he held perfectly still while I zipped him into the bag and carried him up four floors to my room. At thirty-five pounds, about average for an Australian Cattle Dog (also known as a Queensland heeler), Blue's weight was awkward but not prohibitive, and I'd been smuggling him into hotel rooms since he was a fluffy gray puppy. Now he was fourteen years old and then some, and I hadn't been willing to abandon him, even for a few days. Who knew when they would be his last?

I sat on the bed for a few minutes, rubbing the old dog's head and taking it all in, then switched my eyes to the clock. Five-fifteen P.M. I was due to meet Joanna at five-thirty. Time to get ready.

A glance in the mirror made me decide quickly that the chambray shirt, Wrangler jeans and tennis shoes I'd worn for the drive up here were much too casual and crumpled for dinner at a nice restaurant and a night out gambling. Choosing a cream-colored silk blouse that I loved, I pulled on some clean dress jeans and slipped my feet into soft doeskin flats. Adding a string of fresh-water pearls, I evaluated myself as I brushed out my rambunctiously wavy dark hair and confined it in a silk cuff. I decided that a little blush and lip gloss and I'd do.

Giving Blue's head a final rub and telling him to be a good dog and be quiet—barking would get him kicked out of the Foresta for sure—I turned on the TV, hung a Do Not Disturb sign on my door, and headed down the stairs to the hotel coffee shop.

The place proved to be all mirrors and chrome, crowded with so many green plants and their reflections that it looked like a confusing jungle. It took me a moment to orient myself, and while I was trying to decide which of the arched entrances were real and which were illusions, I heard a low-voiced "Gail," from off to my right.

Joanna Lund, who had been my closest friend at vet school, and whom I hadn't seen in three years. I slid into the booth across from her, my smile of greeting masking a look of curious appraisal.

Scandinavian, small, and slender, Joanna had always seemed uninterested in her high-cheekboned good looks when we were in college together. She chopped her blond hair short and didn't fuss with it, wore no makeup, and dressed exclusively in jeans, boots, and man-tailored shirts. Of course, she still looked wonderful, but it was obvious that wasn't the point.

Joanna and I had never engaged in a single conversation that I could remember on clothes, diets, hair styles, or men, subjects that I, like most women, have done my fair share of chatting about. Joanna and I talked exclusively of horses and their health problems. She had determined to become a horse vet when she was fifteen and she'd pursued her goal with a single-minded intensity that excluded men and, to a large degree, friends.

In fact, it was her intensity that had drawn us together. She seemed to be the one person in my class at vet school who, like me, was driven by a need to achieve that rendered boyfriends, parties, and general carousing irrelevant. My parents were dead, and Joanna's were divorced, poor, and uninterested in financing her schooling. We both worked hard as waitresses, had grants, lived in the same crummy apartment building, and studied for all we were worth. It made a bond.

"Gail, you look great." Joanna's smile seemed tentative.

"Well, thanks," I said, pleased and slightly confused. It was unlike the Joanna I remembered to mention looks. "You, too."

She shrugged off the compliment and asked, "So what have you been doing?"

"Slaving away. This is my first vacation in years."

"Are you still working for Jim Leonard? I've heard he's a real slave driver."

"Yeah, I am. Do you know Jim?"

"I've met him, years ago. I have an aunt who lives in Santa Cruz."

"I didn't know."

We smiled at each other again; I was registering little details

3

that hadn't struck me immediately. Joanna's blond hair was still short, but now it was cut in a neat wedge. She still wore a tailored shirt, but this one was a soft pink that flattered her fair skin, and it looked expensive, as if it had come from a designer, rather than the men's department of the nearest discount store. There was a gold locket at her throat, and I thought I detected signs of the same slight application of blush and lip gloss that I used myself. Joanna had changed, after all.

I wondered suddenly why our estrangement since vet school had been so complete. We'd called each other on the phone a couple of times in the last few years; that was it. I knew only that she was practicing as a vet in Merced, a town in California's Central Valley; she knew I lived and worked in the coastal city of Santa Cruz, where I had been born and raised. Perhaps our friendship was based so exclusively on the struggle to survive vet school that there was nothing left of it when that ordeal was behind us. At this point, after three years out in the real world, we were virtual strangers to each other.

I was about to break the rapidly growing awkward silence and ask her what was new in her life, when a familiar booming voice greeting someone in the front of the coffee shop caught my attention. It caught Joanna's, too, and we both stared at a tall man clapping a seated diner on the shoulder.

"Isn't that Jack Hollister?" Joanna sounded slightly awed.

"Who else?" I was less awed, mostly because I knew Jack a little. In point of fact, everybody in the livestock business in central California knew Jack Hollister, or knew of him. Jack was a living legend.

As far as I was aware, he was the only person who had ever put himself through vet school on the money he made riding bulls and broncs on the rodeo circuit. To top that off, he had parlayed the money he made as a horse vet into ranch land, and had invested so successfully that he'd become a modern-day cattle baron. Nowadays he was mostly retired from veterinary work and spent his time going team roping and keeping tabs on his various properties.

Jack had been born and raised in Santa Cruz on a small family ranch that he still called home, and until Jim Leonard, my boss, had moved into the area, Jack was the only horse vet in Santa Cruz County. He still did occasional work for old-timers who "wouldn't use anyone but Jack," and I sometimes ran into him in his professional capacity.

More often, I ran into him at ropings. My steady boyfriend, Lonny Peterson, was a team roper and had been teaching me the sport. In the last few months I'd attempted a little low-level competition, with no great success as yet, but I was having fun and enjoyed going.

Realizing that Jack had spotted me at my table with Joanna, both of us staring right at him, I smiled and said, "Hi, Jack."

"Well, Gail McCarthy, how are you? And how's Lonny?" Jack's big smile improved his still handsome face as he approached us. In his late fifties, he looked a bit like a raw-boned, rough-edged Ronald Reagan. He had the same square-shouldered frame, the dark hair that was magically ungrayed, and the strong jaw. At six foot plus, though, he was a bigger man, and there was something tougher, more elemental, in the line of his mouth. The combination of boyish charm in his coffee brown eyes and an air of patrician nobility he seemed to carry naturally could be very winning. Jack was a favorite with the ladies.

"Lonny's fine. He's coming up in a couple of days to ski with me. Do you know Joanna Lund? She's a horse vet, too. From Merced?" Seeing that Jack clearly didn't, I added, "Joanna, this is Jack Hollister."

Jack and Joanna greeted each other with mutually interested smiles. Uh-oh. Jack always had a pretty girl on his arm and something about Joanna struck me as vulnerable. The expression in her eyes, maybe, combined with the slight attempts at a more feminine appearance. At any rate, I hoped she wouldn't bruise herself on what I thought was the impervious rock of Jack's charm and reputation.

"Mind if I join you?" Jack asked as he began folding his tall frame into my side of the booth.

"Of course not." I moved over obligingly, although Jack's sitting down with us wasn't at all what I'd had in mind. Joanna looked pleased, though.

"So, have you girls been to this deal before?" Jack addressed the question to both of us, but his eyes stayed on Joanna. I thought how typical it was of him to call us girls in that unthinking no-offense-meant way. Jack was of an era and a school that taught that to call a woman a girl was to give her a compliment.

I didn't mind, actually. I'm as resentful as the next woman at a genuinely derogatory attitude on the part of a man, but Jack and his old-fashioned sort of manners didn't bother me. I happened to know that he was as willing to accept a competent woman as a team roping partner as he was a competent man.

"No, I haven't." Joanna answered the question that was obviously meant for her, and I sat back and watched the two of them engage in a tentatively flirtatious conversation as I ordered a cup of coffee from the waitress. In the course of his talk, Jack revealed that he'd been to this convention for every one of its twelve years of existence and, naturally, knew all the hot night spots around the lake. I got the impression that the night life and the skiing were what he came for rather than the lectures, but then, I reminded myself, were any of us so different?

Joanna's pleased look intensified as they talked; she asked his opinion of Henry's, the Foresta's upscale restaurant, where we were planning to go to dinner. Jack liked Henry's, but his favorite spot was apparently a place called Nevada Bill's, about which he waxed enthusiastic. He seemed to be on the verge of inviting us to join him, and Joanna looked receptive. Oh shit, I thought. Exchanging what I'd hoped would be a cozy chat with her for the role of odd man out was not an idea I was enamored of.

When a tall, bald man with a beak of a nose walked up to our table and greeted Jack—and Jack, with a "Good to see you made it, Art," got to his feet and departed—I was sincerely grateful.

Joanna raised apologetic eyes to my face and said, "He's nice."

"Yes, I suppose so. Joanna," I hesitated. I hadn't really talked to Joanna in three years and even before that we'd never spoken about men. Still, she had that fragile air. I plunged on. "Jack's sort of a lady killer, if you know what I mean. He seems to have a different girl every month or so. Just thought I ought to warn you."

Joanna didn't seem to be registering the warning. "He's been married a couple of times, hasn't he?"

"Yeah. Three times. The first two were before I knew him, but I've met the last one. Tara. He ran around on all of them, or so I've been told, and he certainly ran around on her."

Once again the negative import of my words didn't seem to bother Joanna any. "He's divorced now?"

I shrugged. "Yep."

Abruptly, as if realizing that her sudden preoccupation with Jack Hollister at the moment of our reunion verged on rudeness, Joanna closed the subject. "I'd like to get to know him better." Then she stood up. "Ready for dinner?"

"Let's go."

TWO

At eleven the next morning I was on the ski slopes. Dinner at Henry's had turned out to be wonderful, the subject of Jack Hollister was not mentioned, and Joanna and I had played blackjack together afterward in amiable companionship. I was aware of a certain distance in her, a sense that her attention was not really focused on me, but after three years' separation I had no expectations and certainly wasn't offended at any lack of intimacy in our relationship.

She'd confided this morning at our lecture that Jack had asked her out to dinner tonight, and I'd kept my mouth shut (this time) on my opinion of him as a romantic attachment and made plans to have my own dinner with a couple of guys who had also been in our class at vet school. They were friendly and seemed to want to discuss nothing but various case histories; dinner at an Italian restaurant nearby sounded pleasant and harmless.

I was on my own now, though, a state I relished. On my own, on my skis, on a mountain. On the slope of a mountain, in fact, that overlooked Lake Tahoe. The lake was a picture-postcard blue this particular winter morning, surrounded by a black and white tapestry of snow and pine trees. And overall stretched that endless, deep blue Sierra sky.

Tahoe really does look like some kind of a jewel, I thought. As an image it was probably overworked and outworn, but the scene was so spectacular it reduced me to clichés. Giving up all attempts to find words for it, I pushed off and skied down the slope, losing myself in the flow of motion and speed, the thrill of pushing my limits. It was wonderful to be on skis again.

A few more breathless minutes and I made a sliding turn and edged my way into the lift line, glancing with automatic curiosity at the two women I ended up next to—a flamboyant creature in some sort of metallic gold overall, and one in hot pink stretch pants and a chartreuse jacket. Both had skis that were color-coordinated with their clothing.

I provided a definite contrast, as my own ski gear was func-tional, not decorative, and dated from my graduate student days. The university was a mere two hours from the ski slopes, and skiing was the one luxury I had occasionally allowed my-self. I had skis, boots, and poles—all ex-rental stuff that had been on sale at a price I could afford, barely. The rest was wool pants that were baggy and comfortable but not particularly stylish, a fuzzy beanie, and a shelled pile jacket, and I felt slightly out of place as I gazed around.

More women in tight-fitting, color-coordinated outfits were all around me, thronging the lift lines and the deck of the lodge. In defiance of the cold, they were mostly hatless, their hair arranged in fetching styles I'd hardly bother with if I were going out to dinner, let alone tumbling through the snow.

Ah well, don't be so critical, Gail, I told myself. So they have different objectives than you. So what? At thirty-three I was finding I was less and less sympathetic to the youth-and-beauty-oriented culture I seemed to live in; I had to remind myself fairly frequently not to be judgmental.

I was at the front of the lift line now; to my relief no other single appeared to join me and I scooted onto the moving chair and prepared to ride up the mountain in solitary splendor.

And it was truly splendor. As the chair topped the first rise Lake Tahoe was spread out before me once again, jewel of the Sierra. And the mountains themselves. The Sierra Nevada, the range of light, as John Muir had called them. I only knew that nothing I'd ever seen approached these mountains for sheer loveliness. Steep, rough-edged, spiky with silvery granite in the summer, softened by the white, powdery snows of winter, studded with vivid blue lakes and sunny green meadows, they were God's chosen garden.

I was so lost in the view that I had to scramble to get organized when the moment came to get off the lift. One of my nightmares has always been to pile it up as I edge out of the chair and end up lying in the snow in a tumble of skis and poles while the whole ski lift comes to a stop and people behind me, halted in midair, glare balefully down at my prostrate form.

Once again, though, I managed to scoot to the edge of my chair and disembark down the steep exit ramp without tangling up. After a moment to rearrange myself, I started off down the slope, marveling, as I often did, that these big clumsy appendages attached to my feet, when put into motion, could suddenly invest me with the speed and freedom of a bird. In fact, as I swooped back and forth down the snowy hillside, the chill wind brushing my face while the brilliant sun dazzled my eyes, I felt as I imagined a hawk might feel, soaring in great, gliding crescents across the sky.

I spent several hours repeating the thrill until, at around two o'clock, my legs began to protest, reminding me that I hadn't been skiing in three years. Making my way back to the hotel after a leisurely *keoke* coffee in the ski-lodge bar, I felt satisfyingly exhausted. I walked Blue, took a quick shower, put on jeans and a wool sweater and headed out the door for lectures and dinner with no presentiment that disaster was about to overtake my vacation.

It wasn't until seven-thirty the next morning that I got the first inkling. I was listening, chin on hand, to a lecture on equine eye problems; the lecturer was an extraordinarily knowledgeable man, and an even more extraordinarily dull speaker. Despite the fact that the material was fascinating, it was hard to keep my eyes open.

I'd already noticed that both Jack and Joanna were missing from this lecture, a circumstance that seemed suspiciously suggestive to me, but I refrained from mentioning it to Larry and Rod—last night's dinner companions—feeling virtuous at my own restraint. My smug complacency vanished a second later when a woman entered the room and handed the speaker a note, which he read aloud.

"Will Dr. Gail McCarthy please come to the desk to receive an emergency phone call."

Oh shit. Oh my God.

I tried to keep a semblance of composure on my face as I bolted from the room, various horrible emergencies presenting themselves to my mind. Lonny had died in a car wreck, Gunner or Plumber (my two horses) had colicked and died, my house had burnt down. Fear twisted my bowels as I picked up the phone, but the speaker wasn't Lonny, or some minion of the law, it was Joanna.

"Gail, please, I need you."

At least that was what I thought she said; Joanna was incoherent. She seemed to be choking and crying and talking all at the same time, and I had to ask her twice to repeat herself.

"Just come," was all she would say. "Room 331."

I hung up the phone and headed for the stairs, sprinting up them as fast as my tired legs would propel me. Joanna's room was on the third floor; I was certain I could beat the elevator.

When I knocked on her door two minutes later I was gasping for breath, but Joanna didn't seem to notice. She wore a baggy terry cloth bathrobe, her hair was uncombed and tangled, and there were tear streaks on her face. Joanna did not look as if she'd just spent a happy night in the sack, she looked like hell, and obviously felt worse.

Sitting her down on the bed, I put an awkward arm around

11

her shoulders and tried to sound soothing. "What's the matter, Joanna? Whatever it is, I'll help."

This didn't elicit any response except "It's too much."

"Is it Jack?" I tried. Judging by her response, it was Jack. She buried her face in both hands and wept.

"Please, Joanna." I was starting to feel a little distraught myself. "Tell me what's wrong. Did you sleep with Jack?"

It seemed a logical question under the circumstances, but it inflamed Joanna. "No," she half screamed, "I did not, and I didn't want to, either."

"Okay, okay," I said pacifically. "So what's wrong?"

Her own anger seemed to help Joanna regain some control. She sat up straighter and swallowed the next sob. "No, I didn't sleep with him," she said forcefully, "and I didn't shoot him, either."

"Shoot him? Did he treat you that badly?"

Joanna gave me a sideways look out of wet eyes. "You don't understand, Gail. Jack Hollister's dead—and they think I killed him."

THREE

Dead?" I repeated stupidly. "Jack's dead? How?"

"Someone shot him. Oh God." Joanna sank back with a sound that was half a choke, half another sob. "It's too much."

"Come on, Joanna." I gave her shoulders a hard squeeze. "Pull yourself together. If you don't tell me what happened, I can't help. Talk, don't cry. Why is it too much? Surely nobody really thinks you killed him?"

My mind was roving wildly now, trying to imagine any sort of circumstance that would lead to Joanna shooting Jack Hollister, but none seemed possible. I couldn't really believe Jack had been shot; he simply wasn't the kind of person to be the victim of violent crime.

Joanna was talking, finally; I tried to focus in on her words . . . "It's Todd, really, not Jack."

I'd missed something here. "Todd? Todd is the person who's shot? Not Jack?"

"No, no. Todd's the reason it's too much."

Joanna seemed to have recovered some of her composure—maybe she'd sobbed the hysteria out of her system. She kept talking, anyway, and slowly the whole sad story of Todd began to emerge.

Todd was Todd Texiera, apparently, a cowboy on the biggest ranch in Joanna's part of the foothills, and the apple of every Merced County woman's eye. To hear Joanna tell it, anyway. Joanna had met him on a call out to the Hacienda Ranch, and he'd obviously charmed the socks off of her.

The socks and everything else, in short order, it appeared. No matter that Joanna seemed to know he'd already loved and left a dozen other women she was acquainted with, she'd hopped right into bed with him, sure that this time it was different.

Only, of course, it wasn't, and Todd Texiera had left her as he'd left everybody else. About a month ago, it seemed. Left her and proved entirely resistant first to demands and then pleas that he move back in and "work it out." Joanna had been desperate.

Little by little I glimpsed the demeaning straits to which she'd reduced herself. She'd tried to dress more fetchingly to get his attention, she'd invented numerous imaginary reasons for calls out to the Hacienda Ranch, she'd called him constantly. All of which he'd ignored.

He was always pleasant, Joanna said, and sometimes he'd tease her, just the way he used to, so she was sure the feeling was still there.

Fat chance, I thought but didn't say. I recognized Todd Texiera's type from her description and I would have bet my life savings he already had another girl in tow and had no intention of returning to Joanna.

"What about Jack?" I prodded gently.

I'd suspected her interest in Jack had been along the lines of a rich boyfriend, possibly even a rich husband, but it seemed I was wrong. Joanna had wanted to acquire Jack out of an even less noble motivation—she wanted to make Todd Texiera jealous.

"Everybody knows Jack Hollister," she said. "I thought maybe Todd would find out I was dating him."

It was a pathetically revealing statement, and I cringed for her. Not to mention I was sure it wouldn't have worked. The Todd

Texiera types were not susceptible to that sort of game playing. They were the ones who intended to hold all the strings.

"And now you say Jack's been shot and they think it was you? Who are they? The police?"

"Yes." Joanna looked like she was ready to cry again; talking about Todd had calmed her, talking about Jack's murder seemed to do the reverse.

"Come on," I urged her, "tell me what happened, so I can help." If that's possible, I added to myself.

"We went to dinner," she began, obediently composing herself with an obvious effort, "at this place called Nevada Bill's."

It was a combination restaurant, dance hall, and casino, it seemed, small, and relatively elegant. It was also a multiroom sort of an affair—card rooms here, barroom there, slot machines over there—with a balcony overlooking Lake Tahoe. Sometime in the latter part of the evening, after they had finished dinner and were gambling, Joanna had lost track of Jack.

"I just wandered around looking for him for a while; I wasn't particularly worried. Then it got later, and I started hunting for him. I couldn't find him anywhere and it was late and I was tired. I thought he'd found some other woman and ditched me." Joanna choked back another short sob. The imagined rejection still rankled, apparently.

"I finally decided I'd better call a taxi and go back to the hotel. Then I realized I'd lost my purse. I hunted through the whole place again, this time for the purse, though I kept an eye out for Jack, too. I didn't see either one. I had some money stuffed in my pocket to gamble with, so I had enough for the cab. I asked the man at the front desk to call me if anyone turned in my purse and gave him my name and room number here. Then I left.

"The next thing I know is the phone is ringing at six this morning and it's the cops. They told me Jack had been shot; they found his body in the lake, they said. And my purse was out there on the deck they think he fell from."

"Have they been here?" I asked her.

"Not yet. They told me on the phone to stay in my room and a detective would be here to talk to me. After I hung up"—Joanna looked at me appealingly—"I just couldn't stand it. My whole life is falling apart."

It made sense in a way. Todd Texiera had probably been Joanna's first lover. Who knew what irrational impulse had led her to choose a lethal charmer, but it was clear the result had been devastating. Balanced as she was on the fragile edge of control and desperation, the notion that she might be a murder suspect really was too much.

"Washoe County Sheriff's Department." The voice on the other side of the door was quiet and unaggressive, as was the knock, but we both jumped as guiltily as co-conspirators and stared at each other. Joanna's eyes were wide with fright, and her disheveled appearance was exactly what I might have imagined the perpetrator of a violent crime would look like the morning after. She had, I supposed, a motive of sorts. Distraught over Todd Texiera, she propositioned Jack on the rebound and was rejected. Hell hath no fury, etc.

All these thoughts flashed through my mind as I looked from Joanna to the door. Too late to have her change into some clothes, too late to warn her to say nothing about her disastrous love affair. With a whispered "Just answer the questions," I got up and opened the door.

The man who stood in the hallway met my eyes and said, "Ms. Lund?"

"No, I'm her friend."

He looked less than pleased for the merest fraction of a second, then said, "Detective Claude Holmquist."

"Dr. McCarthy," I answered firmly. "Dr. Lund is waiting for you." I laid a little extra emphasis on the "doctor" as I held the door open for him, thinking that this was going to be easier than I'd expected.

Detective Claude Holmquist was not an intimidating man. Small and narrow framed, he looked to be about forty-five, with a receding hair line and a Nordic face. In Joanna those Scandinavian genes had produced a snow-queenesque beauty; in this man they'd created a rabbitish look—his long nose, almost lashless pale eyes, and thinning, faded hair were innocuous at best.

Joanna faced him with more composure than I'd expected; she still looked red-eyed and distressed, but her demeanor was calm. I crossed my fingers it would stay that way.

In response to quiet questions from the detective, Joanna retold the story I'd just heard. The man gave no sign, either verbally or in his facial responses or body language, of what he thought. Unaggressive neutrality was the only quality he displayed. I began to revise my first impression.

"And you, Dr., uh, McCarthy?" He turned those slightly watery eyes on me. "Can you add anything?"

The question was ambiguous, deliberately so, I supposed. He watched me passively; nothing could have been less threatening than the slight sideways tilt of his head, yet I had the strong impression I needed to choose my words carefully.

"Dr. Lund and I are friends and she called me up here this morning as she was upset—naturally."

No response from the detective.

"I should probably tell you that I knew Jack Hollister, Dr. Hollister, slightly, better than Dr. Lund did. In fact, I introduced them a couple of days ago, here at this convention."

Again, no response, just a gentle inclination of Detective Holmquist's chin.

I plugged on. "Jack Hollister is from Santa Cruz, my hometown. He and I are both horse vets, and we both participate in team roping, so I've run into him quite a bit."

"Team roping?"

"It's a sport. A rodeo event. Roping cattle from horseback."

"Ah yes." Claude Holmquist nodded. Again I had no sense what he thought of team roping, of me, of this case, of anything at all. "Why do you think he was killed?"

No inflection in his voice. Just a simple question. I thought about it. "Are we assuming he was murdered, then? It wasn't suicide?"

"Do you have a reason to think he would shoot himself?"

I stared at this man, wondering if he might possibly represent the epitome of the give-no-information-away school of bureaucratic thought. "No," I said finally, "I have no reason to think he would commit suicide. I was wondering why you seemed to assume he'd been murdered."

Detective Holmquist gave the faintest upward twitch of the lips and said nothing.

Since he clearly wasn't going to tell me what evidence he had, or anything else for that matter, I took a deep breath and tried again. "Okay. As far as I know Jack Hollister had no reason to kill himself or be killed by anyone else. He wasn't the type, if you know what I mean. My first reaction when Joanna told me was, that's impossible. Jack was successful, cheerful, and easygoing; that's the impression he gave, anyway. I didn't know him well enough to know if he had any serious problems under the surface."

Detective Holmquist nodded slightly. We were all quiet. When the silence had lengthened to the point of stiffness and it was apparent Joanna and I were not going to volunteer anything more, he spoke. "I'll take down the names of anyone you think we should be in touch with and then get back to you. Would you two be able to wait here for me?"

It was phrased as a request, but I didn't bother to suggest any other program. The alternative was probably waiting around in some police station.

I gave him the name of Jack's foreman and that of his most current ex-wife, Tara, and left it at that. I couldn't remember, if I'd even known, the names of Jack's previous wives; no doubt the police could discover them.

Detective Holmquist departed with this information and a promise to return shortly and left Joanna and me alone.

She was huddled in a straight-backed chair, the hunch of her shoulders and droop of her head conveying her feelings more clearly than any words could have done. She'd remained absolutely silent while the detective had questioned me and she still said nothing, just stared vacantly at the blank gray screen of the silent TV set.

"Joanna," I said tentatively. "Why don't you take a shower and get dressed. You'll feel better."

She shook her head.

I walked over and put a hand on her shoulder. "Joanna, come on. This isn't the end of the world. I know you didn't kill Jack. It will all get straightened out."

"It's easy for you to say." Her voice was a mumble. "Who's going to straighten out the rest of my life?"

"Joanna." I was getting exasperated, tragedy or no tragedy. This new Joanna seemed very unlike the person I had known in vet school, and wasn't someone I found myself liking. I wondered briefly if it was true that we all hit some kind of major life change around the age of thirty, the boundless, somewhat mindless enthusiasm of our twenties smashing against the inexorable wall of mortality. Certainly it was true that several people I had known had changed radically around thirty, some lapsing into what appeared to be inertia and depression, others shifting from freewheeling liberals into aggressive conservatives. Joanna seemed to have changed from a hardheaded career woman into a piece of soggy toast.

Come on, Gail, she's afraid she might be charged with murder, I reminded myself, and tried again to be sympathetic.

"Losing what's his name, Todd, isn't the end of the world, either," I said, I hoped kindly. "We've all been dumped. Life goes on. You've got your work. You'll meet somebody else."

"No, I won't. Todd was the only man I've ever loved, the only man I've ever slept with. Am I supposed to just go ahead and forget him?"

I felt stymied. I'd outgrown this sort of obsessional, I've-got-a-crush-on-somebody-who-doesn't-care-about-me love, or at least I hoped so, but I could still remember what it felt like. It was at the heart of all the he-done-me-wrong country-western songs, and was certainly not peculiar to Joanna. It was, in fact, the glorified romantic love of novels. I wasn't sure how to say I thought it was stupid.

"Joanna, I know you love this guy, but if he doesn't love you, or doesn't treat you with respect, then I think you ought to shut him right out of your life, no matter what it costs you. Don't kid yourself, it will never work out. Wait till you run into someone who loves you as much as you love him."

My God, I sounded like a second-rate advice columnist. Joanna looked singularly unimpressed. She stared at the blank TV screen and wouldn't look at me.

I tried again. "Okay, I know it sounds stupid, I know you think your life is ruined, but would you please, please just for now forget about Todd Texiera and try to remember anything you can about last night that could help explain what happened to Jack."

"Gail, I don't know. I didn't even know the man. I can't help it if he got himself killed last night. I didn't have anything to do with it, that's all I know." Joanna got up. "I think I will take a shower now."

She brushed past me into the bathroom without a word or a look.

Great, just great. I'd alienated her completely. What the hell was I doing here, anyway? I'd constituted myself Joanna's friend and protector, I was inextricably involved as far as the detective was concerned and for what? For the sake of a woman who was acting like an idiot.

Well, I could hardly abandon her at this point. Still, I felt the need of someone to lean on myself. And there was someone, I realized a second later.

Lonny. Lonny was driving up here today, would be arriving around dinnertime. My own romantic attachment, a considerably happier one than Joanna's. The very thought of him cheered me up. Tonight, I promised myself, tonight I'll tell all this to Lonny.

FOUR

Tonight seemed to take a long time in coming. We were questioned two more times by Detective Holmquist and spent the hours in between staring at the TV and eating a room service lunch. Joanna and I seemed to have entered a state of armed truce. She maintained a somewhat formal politeness and I refrained from asking her any more questions. I had apparently failed her in my assigned role of friend and confidante, but I wasn't sure exactly where I'd gone wrong.

I wasn't sure I cared, either. I was more interested in the progress of the investigation, about which I learned, predictably, very little. Detective Holmquist seemed, on his second and third visits, particularly interested in the way in which I had happened to introduce Jack and Joanna.

That it was entirely a coincidence he seemed not to believe, and his questions repeatedly probed in the direction of, had I arranged it, had Joanna angled for it, had Jack angled for it? None of the above, I told him, but it didn't seem to make an impression. That Jack and I were casual friends, that Jack had spotted me sitting with an attractive woman in the coffee shop and had stopped to chat, probably hoping to be introduced, that all of this seemed to me to be certainly unpremeditated by any of us—this the detective found hard to accept.

Eventually he released me, after getting my assurance that I'd be available the next morning for more questioning. I'd taken awkward leave of Joanna and I virtually ran down the corridor away from her room.

My God, what a mess. And so much for my vacation. But Lonny was still coming and would be here in an hour or so. I hustled Blue down the back stairs in his duffel bag and walked him, lugged him back up the stairs and gave him dinner, then took a shower.

Fifteen minutes before Lonny was due to walk in the door I stood in front of the mirrored closet, naked, trying to decide what to wear. Staring hard at my body, I sighed. In Lonny's presence, with the palpable force of his desire for me reflected in his eyes, I seemed, even to myself, to be beautiful and desirable. Standing here alone was a different story. The woman I saw in the mirror was obviously past the freshness of youth; my breasts were beginning to sag a touch; there was a little extra flesh around my waist. Peering closer, I observed that the lines at the corners of my eyes were just as visible as the last time I'd inspected them.

Ah well. I sucked my stomach in, squared my shoulders, and smiled at myself. I'd do, thank you. I'd do just fine.

Five minutes later I'd clothed my body in black pants and a sea green silk shell that almost matched my eyes, with a black cashmere cardigan unbuttoned over the top. My hair was still damp and curled in wet dark tendrils around my face; I was trying to decide whether to blow it dry or not when I heard a knock.

"Who is it?" And it better not be that detective, I added silently.

A familiar voice said, "It's me," and I smiled and went to open the door.

Lonny stood in the hotel hallway, grinning at me, and before I had a chance to do anything more than look up at him and say hi, he'd enveloped me in a bear hug. Lonny is a big man—

22

six-two and wide-shouldered, with long arms and a barrel chest. His hug was emphatic, and for a moment I felt small and fragile as he crushed me against him. Then he let go and we looked into each other's faces.

"Silk wrinkles, you know," I said mildly.

Lonny laughed. "You're supposed to be glad to see me."

I smiled back at him and held the door open. "I am. Come on in while I finish getting ready."

Blue looked up from his spot next to the bed at Lonny's entrance; recognizing him, he got stiffly to his feet and trundled across the carpet, wagging his stump of a tail in greeting.

"Hello, Grandfather." Lonny bent to rub the dog's head, taking an appropriate amount of time to scratch his ears and his back. I stood and watched him, a silly, fatuous smile forming on my face.

Lonny did that to me; his simplest, smallest gestures touched my heart. The way he laughed, the way he petted Blue, the way he hugged me—they were all slight, illuminated views of the generous, happy spirit that overflowed out of his eyes. He stood up now and I looked at him as if I'd never seen him before—a big man nearing fifty with a vague air of untidiness, a beak of a nose, sandy hair, a slight roll over his belt, and those eyes— wholehearted, intelligent, kind. I am a lucky woman, I thought suddenly, as Joanna and her situation popped into my mind.

"So how are you?" Lonny asked.

"I'm fine, but something bad's happened," I said as I twined my still damp hair into a knot at the back of my neck.

"What's that?"

"Jack Hollister's been murdered."

Lonny's shock and disbelief were reflections of my own; by the time I'd finished a terse recital of the situation, my hair was up, my blush and lip gloss on, and my feet were clad in black suede flats. Fastening my pearls around my neck, I said, "I have no idea if that detective really suspects Joanna or not, he doesn't give a thing away."

Lonny had listened quietly; when I finished he remained silent for a moment. "I guess there's nothing we can do," he said finally. "At least, for the moment. Do you want to drive down to the south shore for dinner?"

The south shore of Tahoe is home to all the ritzy high-rise casinos; the north shore, where we were, has more of a casual air. In point of fact, I enjoyed going down to the south shore once in a while to absorb a brief blast of ersatz glamour, but this evening I had something else in mind.

"How about a place called Nevada Bill's, here in Northshore Village?" I asked.

"Never heard of it." Lonny looked at me, comprehension dawning. "Don't tell me. That's where Jack got killed. Gail, are you trying to poke into this?"

"Are you telling me not to?"

Lonny held his hands up. "No, no. How about, I'm begging you not to?"

I smiled. "Lonny, what harm can it do to eat dinner there?"

"I know you." He grinned back at me. "You'll find a way to get into trouble."

"That's unjust." I pulled a charcoal gray wool jacket out of the closet and stuffed my wallet into a black suede bag. "I'm ready."

Lonny got to his feet with a resigned look. "Lead on, Father Brown."

Lonny drove, as his four-wheel-drive Bronco was better equipped than my truck to deal with the icy roads. We'd chugged most of the way through the little one-street town of Northshore Village, when I saw the sign that said Nevada Bill's. Characteristically, the red neon letters were fifteen feet tall, and backed by some sort of glittering silver material that sparkled vividly in the reflected glow. Nevada Bill's was Nevada all the way.

Lonny found a parking place and we climbed out of the car into the winter night. The street was thick with clumps of frozen snow and slippery with ice. Though better than heels, my flats were vastly inferior to hiking boots, and my wool jacket felt like a layer of tissue paper. Shivering in the ten-degree air, so different from the mild Santa Cruz winter I was used to, I gripped Lonny's offered arm firmly as I picked my way down the sidewalk. Sidewalk was an overstatement, really. At the moment, it was a lumpy track through the slick, hardened snow.

After a city block's worth of hiking—it felt like a hike to me, anyway—we stepped through the door of Nevada Bill's. A blast of chilly air followed us inside, where it was immediately overwhelmed by the central heating. In two short minutes, I was peeling my jacket off.

Nevada Bill's was a typical casino, all maroon and gold, with lots of shiny brass trim. Lit gaming tables were islands of brilliant green baize, crowded with people, noisy with the clink of chips and drinks, the laughter and patter of blackjack in progress. Occasional whoops from the craps and roulette tables jazzed up the smoky atmosphere.

Lonny headed immediately for the nearest blackjack table with an empty chair; he liked to gamble. I wandered around for a while, more interested in orienting myself than in playing cards.

As Joanna had explained, Nevada Bill's was composed of several adjoining rooms. The central one, where I stood, contained the gaming tables. Two open archways at either side led into a room filled with slot machines and into a big bar with a dance floor, respectively. Glass walls at the far end of the casino screened an informal restaurant, and a small, discreet leather-covered door in one wall announced itself on a little brass plaque as the High Desert Room. Judging by the menu posted next to it, this was the elegant restaurant where Joanna and Jack had eaten.

Further wandering on my part located five more exits. A set of stairs going up, it appeared to offices, a hall leading to restrooms and phones, and three doors, all along one wall, that showed, through their windowed upper halves, that they led out onto a long deck. Peering through, I spotted the yellow crime tape cordoning off one end of the deck and realized that it must mark the spot where Jack was thought to have been shot.

I tried to visualize the scene in my mind. Jack, leaning on the railing, smoking a cigarette and staring down into the lake, perhaps, someone pointing the gun at him and firing. The body slumps forward and the killer shoves it over the rail and into the lake below before making an escape. I noticed there appeared to be no exit from the deck other than into the casino. So the murderer had to have come back through this building. Unless he or she went down over the railing?

Turning back to the room, I met the flat, impersonal eyes of the pit boss, watching me from the center of the nearest bank of blackjack tables. After a moment her gaze moved on, and I walked in that direction and sat down at an empty table.

The dealer was a man in his twenties, clean-shaven, blond, wearing the uniform black suit and white shirt and smiling a meaningless smile as he took my money and exchanged it for chips. He shuffled and dealt; I got a jack and an ace—blackjack. I turned the cards over and he smiled, said, "Good job" with a slight Australian accent, and pushed my winnings at me.

I let them ride and he dealt me a seven and a nine; I signaled for another card. It came up a five and I laughed.

"Twenty-one it is." The dealer smiled his pleasant, professional smile again as he pushed more chips in my direction.

I played several more hands and my luck held. I didn't hit twenty-one every time, but I continued to win. In ten minutes I had fifty extra dollars in front of me. Pushing a five-dollar chip toward the dealer as a tip, I asked him, "Did you see the man who was killed here last night?"

Though my tone was casual, his eyes lost their bland expression and lifted to mine with some interest. "No, can't say that I did. But I wouldn't have, you know. We dealers rotate constantly, and we have to watch the play. I don't remember seeing him, anyway."

"He was a friend of mine," I said. "I wondered if anybody saw him go out on the deck."

"Not I." He dealt me another hand, then offered, "You might ask the pit boss. The cops were talking to her about it—that's all I know."

The pit boss had been in my mind ever since I saw her spot me at the door, and I asked the dealer, "Could you call her over?"

"Sure." He took my bet—I'd lost this time—and spoke quietly, without removing his eyes from the table in front of him. "Cher."

She appeared at his side instantly, her face wearing the same flat, impersonal, and alert expression it had when she saw me at the door. It was her job. To watch, to be aware.

"Cher, this lady wants to know about the man who was killed last night."

The woman's eyes shifted directly to my face as she sized me up. Cher seemed an inappropriate name. In her midforties, she was square of body and face, and her light brown suit had clearly been chosen for its conservative formality, rather than its ability to flatter. Her eyes were an opaque mud brown and she wore the sort of regulation makeup—matte foundation, medium rust-red lipstick—that implied she wasn't trying to improve her looks, merely appear conventional.

"What's your interest?" she asked.

"He was a friend of mine. Another friend of mine was with him, and the detectives are questioning her about it."

"That the blonde?"

"Yes."

"What do you want to know?"

"What you saw, I guess. Anything that might help explain how it happened."

Cher regarded me quietly. It was her job to protect the house, and I supposed she was trying to decide if I was a threat. After a minute, she said, "The sheriff took my statement. I don't think it's any great secret. I didn't see the man go out on the deck. He could have gone out any of these doors"—she gestured at the three I'd noticed earlier—"and I probably wouldn't have noticed

27

if he'd gone out the far one. I only watch this area. I did see the blonde go out later. She went out the door you were looking out a moment ago."

"How long was she gone?"

"Five minutes, more or less."

"What did she look like when she came back in? Did you see?"

"I saw. I was watching for her. Not many people go out on that deck in the winter. She looked upset." Cher turned her flat gaze into my eyes. "But she looked upset when she went out the door, too."

I nodded. "Did anyone see the man go out on the deck?"

"No. We asked around, so did the cops. He was noticed in the restaurant and gambling at the tables, but no one saw him go out on the deck. No one that will admit to it, anyway."

I hesitated, but I couldn't think of any more questions, and Cher's gaze had already left me and was roaming through her territory. "Thank you," I said, and she turned away without a word.

I played a few more hands of blackjack, lost most of what I'd won, and started looking for Lonny. Spotting him a minute later, walking between tables, apparently looking for me, I hurried up behind his long-striding form and slipped my arm through his. He looked down at me in surprise and I smiled. "Ready for dinner?" I asked.

"You bet. Where are we eating?"

"How about there?" I gestured toward the unobtrusive door with its posted menu. "The High Desert Room."

"Don't tell me. It's where Jack and Joanna ate."

"Right again."

Lonny smiled and shook his head at me. "Just so long as the food's good. And the wine."

"It ought to be. It costs enough. I had a look at the menu a minute ago."

"Am I buying this dinner?"

"Why, Lonny." I batted my eyes at him. "You did invite me."

"That I did. I wasn't planning on investigating a crime, though. I was thinking about a, uh, romantic dining experience."

"This will be both," I assured him.

"Both, huh? Well, all right," Lonny grinned, "if you pay for half."

"Done," I agreed. "Now come on."

The High Desert Room definitely intended to be elegant. Its degree of darkness alone arrested to that. Everything was very western—leather-covered furniture, wagon wheel chandeliers, oak-framed Charles Russell and Frederic Remington prints on the walls. The menu, as I'd warned Lonny, featured some pricy food and specialized, as you might have guessed, in steak.

I decided on Steak Diane—flambéed right there at the table, so the waiter told me—and Lonny selected us a zinfandel to drink. As soon as I leaned back into my chair and took the first rich, peppery sip, I started to speculate on Jack and Joanna.

Had they enjoyed their meal? Had it been awkward? First dates could certainly be that way. What had they talked about?

When the waiter brought our salads I asked him, "Did you happen to see the man who was killed here last night?"

I could feel Lonny wince, but the waiter rested his gaze on my face and said, "I waited on him."

"He was a friend of mine," I said, "and the woman who was with him is a friend of mine, too."

The man nodded. He was Hispanic, and he spoke with a strong enough accent that I had some difficulty understanding him. "Yes, I waited on them both. They seemed to be having a good time, both of them. This I told the police."

It confirmed Joanna's story. She had been quite clear that she and Jack had gotten along well enough. He was nice, she'd said, though she'd thought him somewhat long-winded. It was only after they'd separated in the casino and she couldn't find him that she'd felt something was wrong.

So, what had happened? What had drawn Jack out on that deck—to his death?

I ate my salad and sipped my wine and tried to make a reasonable show of conversing with Lonny, but my mind was elsewhere. When the waiter brought out an elaborate serving table and began assembling and cooking the Steak Diane in a skillet next to our table, my thoughts snapped back to the present. Lonny watched me inhale the strong garlic aroma appreciatively and smiled. "So what have you come up with, Sherlock?"

"I thought I was supposed to be Father Brown," I objected. "And I haven't come up with a thing. Just some questions. The obvious questions—why did Jack go out on that deck? Who went out after him? And why?"

Lonny shrugged.

"It isn't inviting out there," I went on, "not this time of year, anyway. There's snow all over everything and it's freezing cold. You can see where the snow's been beaten down in trails; people obviously do go out there some, but again, why did Jack decide to?"

"With a woman," Lonny suggested.

"Well, in that case it would have had to be somebody he met at the spur of the moment. He would never have invited Joanna to dinner if he knew he would be seeing someone else he was interested in. It would just mess his chances up with both of them. And I can't believe he happened to meet someone while he and Joanna were wandering around gambling, and Jack invited this other woman out on that deck for a romantic interlude. That's pretty quick work."

"Maybe it was someone he already knew. And didn't know would be here."

The waiter served steak sautéed with garlic and mushrooms onto both our plates and pushed his tableside kitchen away. For several minutes we both ate in silence, then I looked up and met Lonny's eyes.

"I just can't really believe it, you know. I can't believe Jack's dead. I think about him eating dinner here with Joanna, just the way we're doing now, and then, sometime in the next few hours he goes out on that deck and someone shoots him in the head, and he's dead. Gone. Over. Finished. We'll never see him again. It seems impossible."

Lonny said nothing. I had a sudden vision of Jack floating face down in the icy waters of the lake. Jesus. Setting down my fork abruptly, I said, "I don't even know what to feel. I just keep thinking it's impossible. That we'll go back to the hotel and there Jack will be in the coffee shop, talking to some old boy and this will all turn out to be a big mistake." Putting my napkin on the table, I got up. "I have to use the bathroom."

The ladies' room proved difficult to find in the semidark of the restaurant. In the end I discovered a corridor with a sign that said Restrooms. The corridor, I noticed, emptied out into the casino, one of the exits I'd noticed earlier. As I walked toward the door marked Women, I noticed something else. Next to a bank of phones was a door that led out onto the deck.

Peering through the windowed top half I could see white flakes drifting down against the darkness; it had started to snow. This door was shielded from the view of the other doors by a small storage shed outside. Jack could have walked out this way and no one would have noticed.

Suddenly I was sure that was exactly what he'd done, though I had no way of knowing. I stared at the snow, which appeared to float upward as easily as down in lighthearted defiance of gravity, and wondered again, why?

Jack had gone to the men's room, perhaps, and wandered outside for a look at the night. I tried to imagine someone following him—a friend, a stranger? Maybe it had simply been a casual mugging gone awry, Nevada's version of Central Park. I wondered, suddenly, if Jack had been robbed.

Sighing, I went into the ladies' room and then rejoined Lonny. "I think I know how Jack went out on the deck," I told him after we'd finished our steaks.

"Gail." Lonny's face and voice were serious. "Why don't you forget about this? Do you have any particular reason to suppose that the police need your help to find Jack's murderer?"

31

Instead of snapping back the sharp reply I had in mind, I hesitated and gave Lonny's questions some thought. "I don't know," I said at last. "I just can't get it out of my mind. A couple of days ago I introduced Jack to Joanna and now he's dead."

"What if Joanna killed him?"

"Why would she? It doesn't make sense. Though I will admit that I don't feel I know her all that well anymore. All this frustrated 'love' for a man she hardly knows and who treated her like shit—it boggles my mind. How could she be so stupid? The Joanna I was friends with in college would never have acted like that."

Lonny shrugged. "People change," he said. "I've done equally stupid things in my time. Are you ready to go?"

"Sure." I smiled at him, meaning to comfort, guessing that his last remark was a reference to his estranged wife, who had left him, he felt, due to his deficiencies. "It's snowing outside," I added.

Lonny's eyes crinkled at the corners. "I like that. Maybe we'll get snowed in. Have to stay in your hotel room all day tomorrow and snuggle."

I laughed. "What about skiing? I thought you wanted to ski."

"Skiing's fine. But I prefer snuggling." Lonny's green eyes conveyed a warmth no words could ever do justice to.

"Well, let's go get a start on it." I stood up and reached for his hand.

FIVE

Snow sifted down all night, intensifying somewhere near dawn into a blizzard. Snug on the fourth floor of the Foresta, wrapped in Lonny's arms, the roar of the wind in the pine boughs outside was a teasing thrill—no threat involved.

First light showed a white and gray kaleidoscope through the window, all whirling snow and opaque sky. I'd barely had time to contemplate this scene, and feel Lonny's hand reach for my breast, when a knock sounded on the door.

"Detective Holmquist here." The voice was as quiet, and as persistent, as I remembered. The man was like the blowing snow, I thought, gentle, but in the end, overpowering.

"Just a minute," I said and hauled myself out of bed.

Lonny shot an annoyed glance at the clock, which read 6:30, and rolled out himself. "I'll be in the shower," he grumbled.

I threw on some sweat pants and a T-shirt and went to the door. "Good morning, Detective."

Claude Holmquist took in my appearance and said mildly, "I was under the impression lectures started at seven."

"Lectures?" I echoed. "Oh, yeah, lectures." I'd forgotten almost entirely the ostensible purpose of my stay here.

I held the door open. "Come on in."

Blue was lying on the floor near my bed and lifted his head and growled as the man stepped through the doorway, then started to get stiffly to his feet. I pointed a finger at him. "You stay there and be quiet." At this he subsided, nose on paws, a baleful stare fixed on Claude Holmquist, but no further overt signs of hostility.

The detective, for his part, regarded the dog without comment, then walked across the room and took a seat in the one chair that wasn't covered with discarded pieces of my clothing.

Seeing that he held a cup of coffee in a paper cup, I didn't offer him any, but went to the machine the hotel had provided, and started the process of making a cup for myself. Lonny's muffled splashing sounded from the other side of the bathroom door; with my back to the detective, I said, "I have a friend staying with me."

When I turned around, his face showed nothing. As far as I could tell, I might have had four or five friends, all cavorting merrily in my bed, and he wouldn't have raised an eyebrow.

He maintained his polite silence until my coffee was ready in its plastic cup and I had cleared another chair and was seated, then settled those mild eyes on my face. "I'd like to ask you a few more questions about your friend Joanna Lund."

"Okay."

"What do you know of her recent life—since she left vet school?"

"Not much. She's a practicing vet in Merced. We haven't spoken to each other very often in the last three years." I tried to keep my voice as neutral as Detective Holmquist's.

"Any romantic entanglements?"

"Only what she told me. During the time we were together here, I mean."

"And what did she tell you?"

At that, I hesitated. Was I going to provide Joanna with a motive for murder? What should I reveal, if anything?

Claude Holmquist caught my indecision and spoke briskly. "Dr. McCarthy, this is a murder investigation. Jack Hollister was murdered; he did not kill himself." The anemic-looking eyes stayed on my face. "He was shot through the back of the head, at an angle which makes it virtually certain he could not have held the gun himself. He was not robbed; his wallet was found on his body with a thousand dollars in it."

There's one piece of useful information, I thought, even as I digested the import of his words.

"We've spoken to the sheriff's department in Santa Cruz County." He was consulting his notes. "I spoke to a Detective Ward, who says she knows you."

"Jeri Ward. Yes."

"She said you would be cooperative."

The words hung between us. I took a swallow of coffee and tried to decide what to say. In the end, I opted for simplicity. "I guess I feel protective of Joanna. I introduced her to Jack, and I truly believe it was a coincidence. I'm ninety-nine percent sure she had nothing to do with his murder, and I'm hesitant to do or say anything that will cast further suspicion on her."

"Ninety-nine percent? Not one hundred?"

"No, not one hundred. I haven't seen her in three years. She does seem to have changed. On the other hand, she has no earthly reason to have murdered Jack."

"These things happen, you know. Anger, perhaps, a spur of the moment rage. Was Dr. Lund in the habit of carrying a gun in her purse?"

"Not that I ever knew. Not in college, anyway. And I'm pretty sure I would have known, if she had one at that time." I hesitated. "Was her purse big enough to have held the gun that shot Jack?"

The detective regarded me levelly. "Possibly," he said at last. "We haven't found the gun yet. I have a feeling it's in the lake. The bullet came from a twenty-two; however we don't know the exact model. We have a suspicion it may have had a silencer on it. However, to answer your question, many types of twenty-two pistols certainly would have fit in Dr. Lund's purse."

Well. If he was willing to tell me this much, he must trust me,

35

at least a little. In another second I realized the other implication of his words. I trust you, now you have to trust me. I was being coaxed to tell what I knew about Joanna.

Claude Holmquist was waiting. Not asking, waiting. The narrow face and inoffensive demeanor masked, I already knew, a keen mind. The very fact that I still wasn't speaking was telling him something.

In the end, I asked him a question. "Has Joanna told you about her love affair?" The coward's way out, my mind mocked me.

"Dr. Lund stated she had a boyfriend, with whom she was currently at odds. She said she dated Jack Hollister to make the boyfriend jealous. She refused to give us his name, and we didn't press her at this time."

"I see." I thought about it a minute and decided I couldn't do Joanna any harm that she hadn't already done herself. "He wasn't exactly a boyfriend," I said.

I told the story of Joanna and Todd Texiera more or less the way it had been told to me, leaving out my own interpretation. When I was done, the detective asked me, "Was it your impression that Dr. Lund was distraught over the failure of this relationship?"

"Yes, I suppose you could say that," I said slowly. "But she still had no reason to kill Jack and, bearing in mind I haven't seen her in three years, I would definitely say she was innocent."

"Why?"

"She seemed so indifferent to the whole issue of Jack and his murder except in the sense that it was adding stress to her already stressed-out situation. She didn't seem truly worried about being a suspect. She seemed completely absorbed in her failed 'romance.' "

Detective Holmquist looked as if he was about to ask me another question, but Lonny opened the bathroom door at that moment and emerged, wearing a towel around his waist. This necessitated introductions, and I was amused at the contrast— Lonny towering over the smaller man, but rendered somewhat at a disadvantage by his semi-naked state; Detective Holmquist slight and frail-seeming, but lent a good deal of dignity by his gray suit.

After ascertaining that Lonny had been in Santa Cruz on the night Jack was murdered, the detective asked him, "How well did you know Dr. Hollister?"

It took Lonny a moment to frame a reply to this question; even before he spoke, I knew what the gist of his words would be. "Not well," he said, "but I've known him for thirty years or more."

At this, the detective pricked up his ears. "Could you tell me about him?"

Lonny sat down on one corner of the bed, holding his towel firmly around him with one hand, and thought for a minute. "Jack and I were part of the same world," he said at last. "We were both involved with livestock and we knew the same people. We knew each other first through rodeo; Jack was riding broncs and I was a dogger."

"Dogger?"

"Bulldogger. It's a rodeo event," Lonny explained. "Basically you jump off a horse and wrestle a steer to the ground."

I was amused to catch a fleeting expression of what?—surprise? consternation?—disturb Detective Holmquist's flawlessly bland face for a split second. Bulldogging was obviously in the same category as throwing Christians to the lions, as far as he was concerned.

Lonny was still talking, explaining as well as he could the way in which rodeo people all know one another, and Jack's prominence in that world. I listened, thinking while I did so that no real image of Jack Hollister as a human being was emerging from the words. The Jack of whom we were all talking, and thinking, was a cardboard figure—the "big man," the local rancher's son who'd "done good."

I tried to conjure up a more intimate version of Jack and found I couldn't do it. I simply hadn't known him closely enough to have any idea what made him tick.

Claude Holmquist was asking Lonny about Jack's ex-wives. "I knew them. Vaguely. I hardly remember the first one. Karen, I think. They divorced a long time ago. When he was in his early thirties."

"Karen Harding." The detective was looking down at his notepad.

"The second one was Elaine. He called her Laney. Blond and beautiful—that's about all I remember. The most recent was Tara. They just divorced—a couple of years ago, I think."

Detective Holmquist nodded. "Can you tell me anything about them?"

"Not much about the first two. Neither of them rode, and the most I knew of either was that she was Jack's wife. My impression was that Laney was chosen for her rather, um, prominent features."

Claude Holmquist permitted himself the ghost of a smile. "And Tara Hollister?"

"Tara was, is, tough. Tough acting, anyway. She's a lot younger than Jack, and good-looking in a hard way. She rides and ropes. Considers herself a horse trainer." Lonny let it go at that.

I agreed with everything he'd said, though I might have added that I couldn't stand Tara Hollister. However, nobody'd asked me.

Claude Holmquist was staring at the pad in his lap. "Bronc Pickett?" he asked.

"He's Jack's foreman." Lonny grinned at the thought of Bronc. "He's an ornery old fart, and a hell of a roper. He and Jack went roping together most weekends. He's been with Jack a long time—as long as I've known them."

"Travis Gunhart?"

"Jack's hired hand. Nice kid." Lonny shrugged. "He ropes a little—he's pretty handy. That's about all I know."

The detective closed his pad and asked what sounded like a final question. "Did Dr. Hollister have any children?"

"No. There was always some talk about that, though. I never

paid much attention. Ropers are as bad as a bunch of old women at gossip."

I rolled my eyes mentally at this statement, but managed to keep my mouth shut.

"Anything else you can add?" Claude Holmquist stood up, looking at Lonny and me in turn.

I shook my head and Lonny said, "No, I don't think so." The detective nodded civilly. "You're both free to go. Someone will be in touch with you in Santa Cruz, Dr. McCarthy, if you're needed."

"All right." I stood up, too, and escorted him to the door. He thanked me for my time as he stepped out into the hallway, his rabbitlike demeanor unchanged, but my impression of the ferret within was strong. I wondered if he'd been grilling Joanna and decided that if he had, she was probably reduced to an emotional pulp at this point. Not an appealing prospect.

But one I needed to deal with, for reasons of curiosity as well as altruism. I wanted to ask Joanna some questions.

SIX

An hour later I was knocking on the door of her room, having showered, dressed, walked Blue, and promised Lonny I'd go skiing with him in the afternoon if the weather cleared. At the moment, it was showing no signs of doing that. Stormy blasts bent the pine boughs outside the windows, and the lake was hidden by a blur of whirling white.

Joanna answered her door wearing the same terry cloth robe she'd been wearing when I left her yesterday. Her hair didn't look as if she'd combed it since then, and her eyes were puffy. She turned without a word and walked back into the room.

Shutting the door behind myself, I followed her and sat down in a chair. Joanna was sitting on the edge of the bed, staring out the window at the blowing snow. I had a feeling she'd been sitting like that for hours, maybe all night. I was trying to decide what to say to her when she spoke.

"I called Todd last night." Her voice was barely audible.

"So what did he have to say?" I tried to keep the what-in-hell-did-you-do-that-for out of my voice.

"Nothing. I told him what was happening to me up here and he basically said that's too bad, honey, and hung up."

I waited, hoping she'd say more.

She raised her eyes from the floor to my face and in the brief turn of her head I saw the pure Swedish structure of her cheekbones, undiminished despite the swollen eyes and tangled hair. "Some girl answered the phone," she said. "I called Todd, at the apartment where he's living, and this girl answered like it was her place. He's already moved in with someone else."

Slow tears had started to roll down her face as she spoke. Unlike the noisy sobbing of yesterday, this was entirely silent. Simply tears running from her eyes.

I didn't know what to do. Perhaps I should have gone to her and held her, but between the estrangement I felt and my own awkwardness, I couldn't bring myself to do it. Any impulse I might have had to offer more advice and platitudes died at the sight of such abject misery.

After a minute she said, "I know you were right, yesterday. I've got to get over him. It's just hard to do." Her wet eyes shifted to the blowing snow outside the window. "I'm sorry I was such an idiot, Gail. I didn't want to hear it—that I ought to give Todd up. He's the only man I've ever loved, the only one I ever wanted. And now he's gone."

"I'm sorry."

We sat in silence while Joanna watched the snow and I watched her. Hardhearted though it sounds, I was wondering how to bring up the topic of Jack and his murder. I was genuinely sorry for Joanna, but it didn't change the fact that someone had killed Jack and she was still a suspect.

She didn't seem aware of this, or rather, as I'd told the detective, she didn't seem to care. Her misery over Todd Texiera had engulfed her to such a degree that I doubted if she cared much whether she was arrested or not.

"Joanna," I said finally, "I don't want you to be arrested for murder. I feel like it's my fault."

She smiled at me through her tears, and for a second I had a glimpse of the old Joanna, the one I'd lived with in college—spunky, intense, stubborn—a woman with a will to survive. More than that, to triumph.

"It's not your fault. I wanted to be introduced to the man. You didn't force me to date him. And you didn't have anything to do with his getting shot. Neither did I." Her tears seemed to be abating. "And I don't think I'm going to be arrested. Not immediately, anyway."

"That's good. What makes you think so?"

"That detective was here last night. After you left. He asked me questions—the same old ones—for hours and hours. But at the end he said I was free to go home tomorrow after the seminar ended. All he said was that I needed to let them know if I left Merced."

So Joanna wasn't a candidate for immediate arrest. I wondered what had drawn Detective Holmquist to that conclusion.

"I don't want to piss you off," I began tentatively, "but how do you think your purse got out on that deck?"

Joanna looked at me oddly; she wasn't crying anymore and seemed composed. Still I crossed my fingers that I wouldn't bring on another onslaught of anger or tears.

"I think Jack took it out there," she said finally. "That detective must have asked me that six hundred times, and I've thought and thought and that's the only thing I can think of. I had the purse at dinner, and I think I had it when Jack and I sat down at a table to play blackjack. After that I don't remember it. What I think happened is that I left it when I went off to try another dealer. Jack stayed at the first table—he was winning and I wasn't—and I think he must have seen my purse and taken it with him when he left. After that, I guess he went out on that deck for whatever reason, and was still carrying my purse when he went."

That sounded reasonable. Now for the tricky part. "Why did you stay out on the deck for five minutes?"

"That's the other thing that detective wanted to know. I guess someone noticed me go out and come in. It sounds stupid, but I'd been looking for Jack a long time by then, and I thought he'd ditched me for someone else and just left. I was, well, upset."

I could imagine.

"When I went out on the deck I wasn't even really looking for Jack. I just wanted to be alone to cry."

"Did you see anything out there, anything at all?"

"No. No one. Not Jack. Not my purse. I might not have noticed the purse, though, if it were sitting in some inconspicuous spot. It was black, and I wasn't looking for it at the time. But I know I would have spotted a person."

If the purse had been there, I thought, unnoticed by Joanna, then Jack had already been shot and pushed over the railing.

"So, after you had your cry and went back into the casino, then what?"

"That was when I noticed I didn't have my purse. I went back to the restaurant, and then to the first table I'd gambled at, but it wasn't either one of those places. And by then I had just had enough. I told the man at the main desk about my purse, called a cab, and came back here. And that's it."

We stared at each other, all the unspoken hostility of yesterday vanished for the moment. Joanna stood up and looked at me with more animation in her face than I'd seen in awhile. "Don't worry about me, okay? I think I'll take a shower and clean up and try and go to that last set of lectures this afternoon. That's what I came here for, after all."

"Yeah, me too. Joanna . . ." I had my hand on the doorknob at this point, but I felt the need to say something to her, something that would bring about a renewed sense of closeness between us. Try as I might, I found I couldn't do it. Like an exhausted marriage, our old friendship seemed empty of meaning. I could find nothing to say except a stilted "I'll see you this evening, then."

She smiled an affirmative and I let myself out of her room, wondering if this was how all relationships died, worn out and feeble. Would Lonny and I eventually come to this point? It struck me that I was singularly ill prepared to answer that question. I wasn't sure I knew what real intimacy was, let alone how, or whether, it always ended.

SEVEN

I left Tahoe the next day. Lonny and I managed to achieve a sunny morning of perfect skiing on the storm's fresh powder, then followed each other home across the Central Valley in the afternoon. He peeled off in San Benito County to have dinner with a rancher he knew; I'd refused his invitation to go along on the grounds that I was already exhausted and needed to be up well before the crack of dawn on the following morning.

Exhausted was the right word. I was mentally and physically beat. Between skiing, and then driving for five hours with Jack's murder constantly on my mind, I felt like a vegetable.

Knock it off, Gail, I ordered as I took the Soquel exit off the freeway and headed up Old San Jose Road toward home. You haven't come up with one useful new idea. Forget this obsession with that damn murder. You're not doing anyone any good, least of all yourself.

It was true. Watching the dark redwood clumps and open meadows of the Soquel Valley slip by outside my windows, I felt like a person slowly waking up from a bad dream. This was home, this was Santa Cruz County, where I'd been born and raised, where I now lived and worked. Tahoe, Joanna, Jack's death, were all part of a strange other world, one that began to recede as I started to focus on my own life again.

In another mile I pulled up in front of my house and smiled. It was still there. A small cabin on the bank of Soquel Creek, the house was built of redwood half rounds; I'd painted it red brown with dark green trim, and it had a little-home-in-the-woods look to it. The "homey" look was enhanced by the tabby cat sitting on the front porch—my most recent animal acquisition.

I'd first seen this cat six months ago, a fluffy tabby with a white chest and paws and a lynxlike face, meowing at my front door. When he'd hung around for two days, meowing steadily, I bought a box of dry cat food at the grocery store and left some on the front porch for him. He ate the food, but continued to meow at the door.

I was absolutely certain I did not want a house cat. Blue was more than enough in the way of animals shedding on the furniture. I left the food out because I felt sorry for the tabby, who was obviously a stray or lost, but I definitely did not want him in the house.

The cat had other ideas. Despite the fact that I kept food in his bowl at all times, and there was a creek full of water right next to the back door, he screamed and screamed in an ever-increasing crescendo. He could screech like a Siamese—raucous, loud wails that were starting to drive me nuts. Two weeks into the siege I'd reached the breaking point.

Sweeping my front porch as he wove between my legs and yowled at me, I lost my temper and swept him off the porch with the broom. The distance from porch to ground was all of two and a half feet, but the cat hobbled off on three legs, packing his right hind foot.

I caught him, of course, and hauled him into the small-animal clinic in Soquel, and, sure enough, he'd broken his leg. So much for cats falling from three-story windows and landing unharmed. Motivated largely by guilt, I'd had the leg cast, had the cat neutered and given his shots, then kept him in a cage (in my bedroom) for the two months it had taken him to heal. After that, there wasn't much point in arguing; he was my cat.

I'd named him Coleman Bonner, after one of my favorite Guy Clark songs, and now, though I might pretend to be resigned, I actually couldn't imagine not having a cat, I'd grown so used to his presence.

He opened his mouth in a loud meow as I got out of the truck; apparently he was convinced that sufficient noise would get him anything he wanted, a not unreasonable point of view, considering his history.

"I'm coming, Bonner," I told him, as I reached back into the cab to lift Blue out. The old dog's stiffness (always worse in the winter) had increased so much in recent months that he could no longer jump in or out of the truck; he had to be carried. He growled softly as I set him on the ground, a ritual complaint at the indignities of age, then licked my hand to show he meant nothing by it.

I watched him snap at the cat, and smiled. It was a token snap, with no intent to damage, more for the fun of it and to show he was boss. Bonner seemed to understand, merely fluffing his tail and scooting out of the way. He wasn't afraid of Blue, and sometimes allowed the dog to maul his neck in a mock "attack," something Blue delighted in.

Following the cat's loudly shouted directions, I let myself into the house, Bonner scampering ahead of me and Blue stumping along behind, and was pleased to see that everything looked intact. I'd just finished redoing the interior (I was hoping to sell it and buy a place with room for horses) and the brand-new sand-colored carpet set off my few pieces of antique furniture nicely. I'd painted the walls and ceiling a soft cream, and stained the old-fashioned window and door frames red brown. Some new bathroom fixtures, and another stain job on the handmade cabinets in the tiny kitchen, and things were looking pretty good.

Pouring myself a glass of chardonnay, I sat down on my preferred end of the couch, Blue at my feet, Bonner in my lap, and stared out my west-facing window. There wasn't much of a view, just a line of trees on a nearby ridge, but I could see that the short winter day was already settling into its early evening. The narrow strip of visible sky was an unsettled dark gray, with a chalky white band just above the horizon. Black, lacy tree branches moved restlessly in the cold light; the radio had predicted a chance of rain for tomorrow. That would make the endurance ride I was scheduled to work a miserable son-of-a-bitch. Nothing I could do about it, though. The ride would go on, rain or no rain.

Considering that Bonny Doon State Park, where the ride was being held, was very steep and the trails could be slippery, rain was going to make it miserable for the competitors, too. Another thought followed. Bonny Doon Park bordered the Hollister Ranch, Jack's family home. Also the place where Bronc Pickett and Travis Gunhart lived.

I stroked the cat and sipped my wine and found my mind right back on the same old track. Bronc had been friends with Jack for more years than I'd been alive. Trav had been with him for as long as I could remember. These were the people who knew who Jack Hollister really was.

I took another swallow of wine. Jesus, Gail, you are a cold-hearted bitch. Did you ever think you ought to be offering them your sympathy, rather than picking their brains?

Dumping the cat off my lap, I went into the kitchen to find dinner. Chili and rice, it looked like, my old standby. At seven-thirty I walked Blue, got my coffee pot ready for the morning, and turned in with my alarm set for three A.M. Tomorrow would be coming awfully soon.

EIGHT

It was two hours before dawn and the sky was flat black, no moon or stars visible through a thick layer of cloud. The wind whipped sharply across the blank open ground of the field where the endurance ride was scheduled to meet. In my head-lights I could see campers, trailers, and tents scattered across the grass; horses were tied to trailers or corralled in little portable pens nearby. Lights glimmered here and there and moving human shapes indicated activity. I parked my truck on an empty strip of grass by a lamp standard and got out.

I almost got right back in. Despite my long underwear and three layers of turtleneck, sweater, and jacket, the icy wind seemed to cut right through me, causing me to shiver instantly. Damn. I'd forgotten my wool beanie, left behind in the bag of unpacked ski gear on my bedroom floor. Small, cold knives of wind were already making my ears ache.

Two women, who had obviously seen my truck with its white plastic multicompartmented bed and drawn the logical conclu-sion, were leading their horses up. One asked if I was ready to do pre-race exams. I nodded my head yes and she handed me her card. Race day had begun.

The pre-ride check, which I was beginning, was an attempt

to ascertain that all horses scheduled to compete were sound and healthy. Each contestant gave me his or her card, and in the pre-race column I marked the categories with a grade of A to D. Categories included soundness, dehydration, mucous membranes, and capillary refill. All of these were indicators of a horse's health and general well-being.

I'd checked about a dozen horses and my hands and feet had gone numb—my ears felt as if someone were drilling into them with a very sharp drill—when I heard a "Hi Gail, you look cold."

Smiling, I turned to greet Kris Griffith, the one person here today that I knew well. Kris was a client of mine and a friend; she'd boarded my horse, Gunner, the first year I owned him, and she and I had lunch together on the rare occasions when I had some free time.

She was also one of the primary contenders in this race; she and her ten-year-old gelding, Rebel Cause, had won the legendary Tevis Cup two years ago and were, from the scraps of talk I'd been overhearing this morning, a good bet to win today.

Kris handed me her card, and I began the process of checking Rebby over. A dark brown gelding, 15.3 hands and a registered Quarter Horse, Rebby was bigger and heavier than most of the other horses, who were predominantly Arabs. In actual fact, Rebby was more of a Thoroughbred than a Quarter Horse; he'd been bred for the track, and his Thoroughbred ancestry made his excellence as an endurance horse a good deal more understandable.

He stood quietly while I felt his legs, checked his gums, and listened to his heart and gut sounds, but danced and cavorted playfully next to Kris while she jogged him out for soundness. Like most of the horses, he was "up"; the early hour, the other horses, the cold wind, and general pre-race excitement made a thrilling blend.

Handing Kris her scorecard with all As marked on it, I said, between chattering teeth, "He looks good. Will you win?"

She shrugged. "Maybe. I've got a chance. That's my main

competition." She pointed at a man leading a gray Arab in our direction. "Jared Neal and Jazz. They've beaten us a couple of times in the past."

"Well, good luck," I told her.

"Thanks." She turned and led Rebby away; I was struck, as I often was, by the intensity of her composure. She seemed calm and poised, yet with an inner fierceness just beneath the surface, a glow that illuminated her pale, plain face.

Joanna had had that quality when I'd known her in college, I thought; it was what had drawn me to her initially. In both women a formidable combination of will and intelligence was masked by a quiet facade. I had no time to speculate on what aspect of my character attracted me to such people, or why two equally strong women had allowed themselves to be undermined by men—in Joanna's case, her ill-advised love affair, in Kris's, an overly dominant husband—as the man pointed out to me as Jared Neal was handing me his card.

Kris's main competition had shoulder-length brown hair in a ponytail, wore black Lycra tights and tennis shoes, and looked as if he could run fifty miles as easily as his horse. The gray Arab packed a lightweight neoprene saddle and a nylon bridle, and both horse and man were hard-muscled and wound tight. Jazz, too, received all As, and Jared Neal led him prancing away.

Two hours later, a cold dawn light suffused the sky, and thanks to me and a fellow vet, Craig Collins, all sixty-odd competitors had been checked in.

I listened to the race organizer—a woman in her sixties who had won every big endurance event there was at one time or another—give the competitors instructions and rules, then grabbed a brief cup of coffee and climbed into my truck to hustle off to the first checkpoint.

Fifteen bumpy minutes later, with the sun coming up over the southeast ridge behind me, I pulled into a level picnic area on the top of Gray Whale Hill. Getting out of my truck, I stood facing the wind, looking down wide, grassy slopes interspersed with brushy areas to the Hollister Ranch headquarters. Jack's family home, just outside the park boundary, was completely visible from my vantage point on the hill. Cupped in a hollow beneath me like a toy farm in a giant's palm, a low, U-shaped adobe house, two smaller houses covered with weathered wooden shingles, three large barns, a shop, a pump house, several sheds and many stout-looking wooden corrals formed a grouping that was deeply reminiscent of an earlier time. A time before tract houses, I thought bleakly.

The ranch and its hollow sat at the end of a gully that emptied from the hills to the sea, the channel of a stream that I could see meandering through the meadow behind the barn. Just below the hollow, the ground dropped off gently, until, not a quarter mile from the ranch yard, the scrubby pasture melted into the sandy verge of a beach.

And beyond that—I lifted my eyes—stretched the endless reach of the ocean. Blue-gray-green today, spattered with whitecaps, shifting and changeful under rapidly moving clouds and sudden rays of thin, early sunshine.

Turning my gaze back to the barnyard, I saw a small figure in what looked like a denim coat and white straw cowboy hat emerge from one of the shingled houses and start across the yard toward the largest barn. Bronc, I thought. Even at this distance he had a certain way of moving—brisk, energetic, a little stiff—that I could recognize. I would go down there and talk to him, I promised myself, as soon as the race was over.

At the moment there was work to be done. Craig Collins and I selected an open piece of level ground for jogging horses, and set our equipment on a picnic table nearby.

A shout from one of the race organizers, "Horses coming," had us all craning to see down the hill where the trail rose into view. In another second Jared Neal and his gray Arab were clearly visible, going at a high lope, all alone, well ahead of the field.

Jared had already reached the checkpoint and was watering Jazz—letting him drink while splashing water on his neck and head—when Kris and Rebby appeared in the distance, accompanied by a woman on a bay Arab. They, too, were moving out, and, like Jazz, arrived at the checkpoint sweaty and steaming.

Jazz, Rebby, and the bay were all walked and watered until their pulse and respiration were down, then Kris led Rebby up to me to be checked.

The dark brown gelding looked good. He was wet with sweat and restive with the desire to be off; his eye was bright and eager. He stood reasonably quietly, though, while I checked his gums, noting that their color was good and the capillary refill was excellent. I pinched his skin and it sprang back quickly—no sign of dehydration. He had normal gut sounds for a horse in the midst of activity and his muscle tone was fine. When Kris jogged him to me he trotted out freely, his feet hitting the ground with an even beat. There was one odd thing, though.

"Does he always travel that wide behind?" I asked Kris. While she jogged him again, I pointed out to her that the gelding seemed to be swinging his hind feet out as he traveled. "Is that just him, or is it different?"

She shook her head. "I don't know. I've never noticed it before. He seems sound, though."

"Yeah, he's sound." I watched Rebby trot again and said, "He's even on both sides." Giving him a B for soundness, I told Kris, "Keep an eye on him, though. I don't remember him being like that before."

I handed Kris her card and turned to greet the next competitor. People were lining up in front of me, and I worked steadily for a couple of hours checking horses in and out. I had time only to note Kris's departure out of the corner of my eye; Rebby seemed to trot out of the checkpoint freely, and immediately picked up the lope, hard on Jazz's heels.

Three hours later, more or less, I was checking the last couple of stragglers who were accompanying the drag rider—an officially designated person who rides last, making sure no one is abandoned on the course who needs help. The "drag" in this case was a fiftyish woman who'd competed in many a race;

today she was just helping out. With her were a young girl on an old horse and a man on a recalcitrant mule.

Both the old horse and the mule were doing okay, medically speaking, but their riders elected to take advantage of the gooseneck trailer parked at the checkpoint by the race staff, and accepted a free ride back to the starting point. The girl was worried about her twenty-three-year-old mount, and the man explained that the mule had already bolted off the trail several times without warning, once rubbing him off on a convenient tree. A long, bleeding cut on his forehead attested to this, and I examined it briefly, gave him some gauze to keep it clean, and suggested he might want to see a doctor.

As he was pooh-poohing this suggestion, with the drag rider remonstrating firmly, the steady clip-clop of hoofs coming up the hill alerted us to the fact that the leaders had now made one lap and were coming in again, having already gone approximately forty miles.

Craning my neck anxiously to see who was coming up the hill, I could hear the mutters from the race crew. "Jared, he'll be in front."

"I don't know, Rebby and Kris beat him last time."

We all stared at the spot where the trail rose into view. Who was ahead?

Jazz and Jared, it turned out, with Kris and Rebby right on their heels. The woman on the bay horse who had been with them earlier was nowhere in sight. Jazz and Rebby were both obviously tired now, shiny wet with sweat and puffing hard; both would take a significantly longer time to come down than the first time I'd seen them.

Kris and Jared Neal were absorbed in cooling their horses. I stretched and ambled over to the edge of the bluff; my feet ached from standing in one place for hours.

Sun warmed my shoulders and glinted off the blue of the distant ocean in dancing pricks of light, mocking the icy cold of early morning. It had turned out to be one of those changeable winter days that we got here in coastal California; one moment the sky was bright and sunny, the next it was darkly gray and threatening rain. A couple of times it actually spit a few scattered drops at us before, once again, the clouds would disappear. I'd spent most of the day taking my jacket off and putting it back on.

For the moment it was shirtsleeve weather. I stared down the slope, thick with clumps of greasewood and occasional stands of live oak, to the Hollister Ranch. The barns and houses sat quietly in the weak winter sunshine, no humans visible. I could see three horses grazing peacefully in the pasture behind the largest barn. What would happen to the ranch, I wondered suddenly, now that Jack was gone?

Someone tapped me on the back and I jumped a foot.

"I'm sorry." It was Kris. "Could you check Rebby now?"

"Sure. So how's it going?" I asked her, as I went over Rebby's vital signs.

"Okay," she said, but she looked doubtful. "Ever since you pointed out to me that he's traveling weird behind I keep thinking he feels funny. But he's not limping."

"No, he's not," I agreed as we jogged the horse. But I could feel the same frown that was creasing Kris's brow on my own face. Rebby was swinging his hind legs outward. It was subtle, but it was there.

"So what do you think?" Kris asked anxiously.

"I don't know what to tell you," I said slowly as I felt up and down both legs and flexed all the joints. "There's nothing obvious here and he's moving out freely. If this was his normal way of going I wouldn't think anything of it. But you don't seem to think it is."

"I sure don't remember him being like this. But he wants to go."

We both stared at the dark brown gelding. Despite being sweaty and obviously somewhat tired, his eye was bright and his expression alert. He didn't look the slightest bit uncomfortable or ready to give up.

I marked him with a C for soundness and told Kris, "It's your call."

She looked down and I could see the struggle on her normally quiet face. Kris was strongly competitive; she wanted to win this race. On the other hand, there was no doubt in my mind that she loved Rebby and wanted to do what was right for him. Emotions tangled; her jaw muscles tightened.

"We'll go on," she said at last. "As long as he feels like he wants to. I won't push him."

I nodded. When she left the checkpoint a few minutes later, following Jazz, Rebby trotted out freely and seemed eager to pick up the lope. Whatever was bothering the brown gelding, if anything, couldn't be bothering him very much, I told myself. Horses that hurt don't move out like that.

On the other hand, Rebby was a horse with tons of heart. "Quit" was not in his vocabulary. No matter how he felt, he'd probably be willing to try and go some more. I shook my head in confusion; the mannerism, lameness, whatever, that Rebby was displaying wasn't something I'd ever seen before. I simply didn't know what it meant, if anything.

Two hours later, I finished up with the last of the stragglers, talked a few brief seconds to the drag rider, then hurried back to the finish line. Most of the competitors were already in camp, unsaddling and feeding their horses, by the time I made it.

I zipped my jacket up to my chin as I got out of the truck and wished yet again for my wool beanie. The clouds had darkened once more and the sharp little wind was chilly with the advance of the winter evening. I hustled over to the area where Craig was jogging horses, wanting to get this over with.

"Who won?" I asked him, as I accepted a race card from a woman with a sorrel saddle-bred gelding.

"Jazz," he said briefly. "Rebby was second."

I nodded and went back to work. By the time Craig and I finished all the post-race checks and gave the best-conditioned award to the bay Arab mare who had finished fifth, Kris had already loaded Rebby up and left. She hadn't even entered him in the best-conditioned class, knowing that his low marks on soundness would eliminate him and anxious, I was sure, to get him home.

Hoping Reb would be all right and thinking I'd call Kris later to find out, I got wearily in my truck and bumped out of the parking lot, looking longingly forward to a glass of chardonnay.

There was still an hour or so of daylight left, though, and the Hollister Ranch was only fifteen minutes away. I'd been out there before on a couple of calls, and I knew my way around the place. It wouldn't take long just to see if Bronc or Trav was home. That's what I told myself, anyway.

NINE

Ten minutes later I was down Empire Grade, past the university, and driving through the many new housing developments on the northern edge of Santa Cruz. Populated largely by university students, professors, alumni, and employees, I assumed. No doubt the developments were a boon to construction contractors, real estate agents, and local merchants, but they were not an asset to the scenery. Slowly but surely the ugly new tract houses and condos were creeping over the ground, encroaching on the open land to the north of Santa Cruz, pushing the city's boundaries ever outward.

It wasn't two minutes after I passed the last stoplight on Mission Street that I turned into the entrance to the Hollister Ranch. The ranch looked peacefully secluded, there in its hollow by the sea, but the nearest tract was less than a mile away. I wondered how long it would be before the old place was finally gobbled up.

I parked my truck in the barnyard and got out. The big buckskin horse Bronc usually rode was tied to the hitching rail, and Bronc himself emerged from the largest barn and came walking in my direction, his arms held wide. I smiled at the sight of him.

A short, feisty character in his sixties, Bronc was crudely flirtatious, hot-tempered, and tougher than nails. He and Jack had always appeared an odd duo, like a terrier and a wolfhound, and I'd often wondered how they ended up together.

"Well, hi there, sweetheart; you finally come to move in with me?" Bronc closed in for a hug, which I gave him, then kissed me on the cheek. "Would you like to step into that house over there?" he whispered in my ear.

I laughed and disentangled myself from his embrace. "Not today, Bronc. I came to say I'm sorry about Jack."

The words made my voice solemn and Bronc's face grew correspondingly stern. "I'm pretty sorry about it myself."

For a moment we were silent. "I know you and Jack have been . . . were," I corrected myself lamely, "friends for years. It must be hard."

Bronc jerked his chin up. "Forty years," he said shortly.

"Didn't you guys used to ride saddle broncs together?" I asked, trying to get him talking.

Bronc snorted. "Jack and I were roughstock riders—bulls, saddle broncs, bareback broncs—we weren't particular. Not like those prima donnas you see out there today."

For a minute he was quiet, staring off across the barnyard, his expression unreadable. "I met Jack when I first went to work for his old man, right here on this place. I was twenty-five and flat broke from riding in the rodeos. Jack was a great big strapping kid of seventeen, just dying to learn how to ride a bucking horse."

"And you taught him."

"I damn sure did. His old man, Len Hollister was his name, hired me to break a string of horses for him. There were twelve of them, all big, strong geldings, anywhere from three to six years old. Never been touched." Bronc spat and cleared his throat. "See, how he came to have them was Len had a studhorse, a soggy-looking yellow horse, the kind of horse you don't see much anymore. He was big and quick, a cold-blooded son-of-a-bitch who would buck your ass off if he could. But he was a ranch horse—a horse you could part cattle on, or rope a steer, or ride forty miles in a day if you had somewhere to go. And his colts were just like him. Big and quick and double tough. "The reason the old man had a dozen of 'em standing around, all unbroke, is he didn't have anybody who could ride 'em. He was too old, and his hired hand was as old as he was, and the kid didn't know one damn thing about starting colts. So Len hired me for the summer to break them all."

"And you stayed?"

"That's right. I broke every one of those bastards and worked my tail off with the cattle besides. The old man liked me. He asked me to stay on."

"Did you teach Jack to ride broncs that summer?"

"I didn't really have a lot of choice." Bronc laughed, his sharp old eyes lit with a memory I couldn't see. "The kid was dying to learn, wouldn't stay away from the bullpen where I worked those colts. I told him he was too big—he should have been a dogger, big men are good for that—but he wanted to ride rough-stock. You never could tell Jack anything."

Bronc seemed to run down at that, the light of his old memories dimmed by the darkness of recent events. I touched his arm gently. "I'm sorry about Jack. You must miss him."

Bronc turned away abruptly and slapped the buckskin horse on the shoulder. "Willy, here, is the last of the old man's line. His mama was an own daughter of the yellow horse—Hondo, we called him."

We both regarded the gelding with appreciation. Of course, I'd seen him before; he was the only horse I'd ever seen Bronc ride. Big for a Quarter Horse, all of sixteen hands, he was dark gold with a black mane and tail and black socks, and had the pronounced black dorsal stripe and zebra stripes on his legs and withers that were typical of buckskins. Despite Bronc's comments about the yellow stud and his ornery disposition, I thought Willy looked kind, and I knew he was a hell of a rope horse.

59

"Willy's got a nice eye," I said.

"Willy's a good one, all right. This sucker doesn't have a mean bone in his body. I had him standing out in the field here until he was four years old, just never had time to ride him. Then one day I got in a little early and saw him standing there and I said to myself, Well, I guess I'll ride the son-of-a-bitch.

"So I took him down to the bullpen and I saddled him and damned if he didn't act like he'd been saddled every day of his life. So I just hung that snaffle bit in his mouth and climbed on. And off he walked, easy as pie."

I smiled and agreed. "Some of them are like that."

I doubt Bronc even heard me; he was rolling now, absorbed in his story, a trait I knew others found tiresome. I enjoyed listening to him, though—his stories seemed to bring another, earlier world to life.

"So after I rode him around the pen a couple of times I just reached over and opened the gate and out we went. I rode him around that little twenty-acre hay field right over there"—Bronc waved a hand at a level area off to his left—"and then I just kicked him up into a lope. He never even humped his back. Two days later I took him on a gather."

He looked back at the buckskin gelding as he spoke and slapped the horse's neck in a gesture of rough affection. He wasn't exactly petting him, not by my standards, anyway, but Willy seemed to take it as meant and neither threw his head nor sidled away, just stood there unmoving, as if to say, "I'm used to the old fart."

Bronc stepped up to the horse and, resting one arm on his back, stood there looking over the buckskin rump across the darkening barnyard. The barns and employee houses surrounded us, hulking silvery-gray shapes in the winter dusk. Even though the natural hollow of the land and the buildings diminished the wind, it was still a long way from warm. In fact, I was shivering inside my jacket, but I wanted to keep Bronc talking.

"Where's Travis?" I asked tentatively.

Travis Gunhart lived in one of the two employee houses—Bronc lived in the other.

"He went to town." Bronc was staring off toward the adobe ranch house, suddenly looking very much an old man. The cold, rapidly dimming light, I wondered, or the fact that his usually animated face was still for once? Bronc had to be, what? Sixty-five? Around that, I thought, though he usually impressed me as looking more like fifty.

"I can hardly believe Jack's gone," he said at last, as if talking to himself. His eyes drifted to the south, where the sea, hidden now in the gathering darkness, murmured endlessly. "There's always been a Hollister on this ranch, ever since I've been here. And that's forty years."

Poor old man, I thought sadly. He's outlived his life. Everyone who mattered to him is dead. Feeling ghoulish, but still wanting to know, I asked, "What will happen to it? The place. Will it be sold?"

Bronc snorted, his old inimitable self in the turn of a second. "Goddamn developers. No, the sons-of-bitches won't get it. It goes to the state."

"To the state," I parroted stupidly. "Why's that?"

"Jack's will," Bronc said briefly. "He left the ranch to the state, to be part of Bonny Doon State Park. Wanted them to preserve it the way it is now. Like the Wilder Ranch and the Coe Ranch."

"Oh," I said blankly, wondering what this meant. "Jack left everything to the state?"

"No, not everything, just this one little old five-hundred-acre ranch. The home ranch, we called it. Jack owned land all over California. All over Nevada and Oregon and Washington, too. But that's all part of the rest of his estate. It's just the Hollister Ranch that goes to the state."

"So who gets the rest of his estate, do you know?"

"Oh, I know all right." It was too dark to see well, but from the sound of his voice Bronc's old eyes were bright. "Jack showed me his will when he made it, right after he got a divorce

61

from that last bitch. A couple of years ago it was." He was abruptly silent.

He was baiting me, I thought. He knew I was curious and so was deliberately withholding the information, just to make me ask.

All right, I'd ask. "So who gets it?"

Bronc held his silence a moment, playing it out, but I wasn't really worried. He liked talking more than he liked not talking. After another second he grinned, his teeth a brief flash of white in the dusk. "His ex-wives."

"His ex-wives. My God. Why?" As the words left my mouth I realized my comment was hardly tactful, but the shock behind it was certainly genuine. How many people left millions and millions of dollars to be divided among their ex-spouses?

"Didn't have anyone else to leave it to, I guess." Bronc's voice was noncommittal.

Why not you, I thought instantly, or Trav, but this time I kept it to myself.

For a second we were quiet. Then I asked, "What will you do?"

"Why, move in with you, of course. If you'll have me." Again the flash of teeth. Bronc laughed. "Naw, honey, I can stay here. Jack wrote it that the state had to let me live here till I died, and anything on the place that's portable—livestock, vehicles, whatever—is mine."

"What about Trav?"

Bronc's face seemed to shut down at that. "He can stay here, too," he said briefly and, I noted, uninformatively.

But my mind was already shifting back to what I saw, suddenly, as the all-important question. "Jack's wives—ex-wives I guess—do they know what they'll inherit?"

"Uh-huh. The damn fool went and told them."

"Why?" I asked, completely nonplused.

"It was Jack's way. He wanted them to know he did right by them. I think he felt guilty. Damn fool."

"Guilty?"

For a second I thought Bronc wasn't going to answer, but then he said, "Jack couldn't have kids, you know. He was sterile." I shook my head. I certainly hadn't known. Was this, I wondered, what Lonny had meant by "talk"? I'd always thought the gossip was about Travis being Jack's illegitimate kid. But somehow I didn't like to come right out and say this to Bronc.

"Well, it ruined him." Bronc was still talking. "He couldn't get it out of his head. I sometimes thought all his running around was on account of that. Either way, I think he never felt he'd done right by his wives, whether because he didn't give 'em kids or he ran around on 'em, I don't know."

"What were Jack's first two wives like?" I asked curiously.

"Well, Karen, the first one, she was a nice girl, a ranch girl. But she couldn't stand Jack's philandering. Maybe if she'd've had kids it would have been all right, but I don't know. She got fat and bitter in just a few years and a few more years later she'd had enough.

"Now Laney, the second one, didn't have a mean bone in her body, but Willy, here, was a little smarter than she was. She lasted almost ten years, but she got tired of Jack playing her for the fool finally; it was just too goddamn obvious. She stuck him for a whole lot of money in the divorce, more than Karen got, by a long shot. Had a smart lawyer, I guess. I hear she lives in a big house down in Capitola now."

Was this a motive, I wondered. Did the long-gone Karen just want her fair share? Or did Laney want more? All of the wives had a motive, since, supposedly, all of them had known about Jack's will. Including Tara, the only one of the three I knew. Knew and detested.

"What about Tara?" I asked Bronc, and got my strongest reaction yet.

"That goddamn Tara was purely a bitch." Bronc spat on the ground to emphasize his words. "I never hated a woman worse than I hated her."

"Do you think she killed him?" It just seemed to pop out of my mouth.

Bronc didn't answer. For a minute he stared at me and then he turned away and untied Willy from the hitching rail. "I'd better get to feeding."

"Bye, Bronc," I called after him as he headed to the barn. "You going to Freddy's tomorrow?"

He stopped for a second and looked back at me. "Might as well."

"I'll see you there," I told him.

"You bet. And if you get tired of that big lunk you're running around with, you just let me know." Bronc chuckled briefly and led Willy into the barn; I could hear the click as an electric light turned on, spilling yellow light out the door to where I stood. Following the broad lit swath to my pickup, I jumped in and cranked the heater up to full blast.

It was black dark when I pulled into my own driveway and got out of my truck. I could hear Blue whining on the other side of the door; I'd left him in the house since I hadn't felt I'd have any time for him in the course of the endurance ride, and he was eager to be let out. Walking him down the steps to the small yard I'd fenced by the creek, I noticed with a pang how stiffly he was moving. Even a year or so ago I would have left him in the yard with its sturdy doghouse, but between age and arthritis Blue couldn't take the cold anymore; the slightest drop in temperature caused him to shiver.

If he lived, this spring he would be fifteen. If he lived. I watched him stump around the yard, then urinate awkwardly by half squatting—he could no longer manage to lift a leg—and a knot twisted in my stomach. Blue looked very old and fragile, and he was getting weaker. Some day soon, the time would come.

I could hardly bear the thought. Blue had been a part of my life for so long I almost couldn't imagine who I would be without him. Was this the way Bronc felt about Jack, I wondered suddenly. As if he himself were incomplete, no longer the same person, now that Jack was gone.

Of course, Bronc hadn't acted very upset about Jack, but then he wouldn't. Men like Bronc felt that to show or even acknowledge emotion was a sign of weakness. Bronc's whole way of being demanded that he deny all vulnerability and be tough and carry on. Yet the old man had been grieving in his own way. I had felt it in my gut, though he'd given no overt signs.

And Travis, I wondered, how was Travis taking it? Bronc said he had gone to town. Was Trav even now at some bar, drinking himself under the table?

Blue stumped up to me and sat, leaning against my leg. I squatted down next to him and put my arm around him, rubbing his chest. He leaned harder, showing his appreciation, but I noticed he didn't smile. That dog "smile," an open-mouthed, happy pant, hadn't been on his face in a long time. Another sign.

I walked slowly up the stairs, accommodating myself to Blue's pace, and let both him and the cat into the house, then went straight to the refrigerator and poured myself a glass of wine. Call me weak-minded, but reminders of mortality always make me want a drink. First that talk with Bronc about Jack, and now the obvious fact that Blue was getting near his end.

At the moment what I wanted was to forget, and I chose the time-honored method. Three glasses of wine, a scanty dinner of soup and bread, and I rolled into bed in the pleasant stupor of mild inebriation, no longer worried about death or anything else.

TEN

At eight o'clock the next morning I was driving down the road to Lonny's, Blue sitting on the seat beside me, alive for one more day, anyway. Turning into Lonny's narrow driveway, I pulled up next to his barn. Automatically my eyes skimmed over his two horses, Burt and Pistol, finishing their breakfast hay in the corral nearest the barn, and moved on to the next corral. There were two horses in this pen, too, one bay, one light brown, heads down, nibbling at the last few pieces of alfalfa. I climbed out of my truck, fetched two halters from the barn, and went to catch them.

Heads lifted at my approach, ears pricked forward. Gunner, the bay, nickered, a deep huh-huh-huh sound, and walked to meet me. A second later Plumber gave his shriller, higher-pitched nicker and followed Gunner in my direction. I leaned on the gate, watching them.

Gunner looked more like one of the Budweiser Clydesdales than the well-bred Quarter Horse he was. His winter coat was especially thick and shaggy and he grew long feathers on his fetlocks, just like a draft horse. With his heavy black mane and tail, big white blaze and high white socks, he would have fit right into the beer wagon team.

66

Of course, I could have prevented all this shagginess by keeping him blanketed and in a stall. But I felt horses were happier living in a more natural way, and in the mild Santa Cruz climate a few oak trees were adequate shelter for animals who had been allowed to grow their winter coats.

So Gunner and Plumber lived here in their half-acre pen on Lonny's property, next to the corral where he kept Burt and Pistol. The pen was built of brand-new metal pipe panels—panels that had, as it happened, eaten up most of my savings account. But pipe fencing is one of the safest and most trouble-free sorts available for horses, and I felt it was worth the investment.

Plumber edged up to greet me as I blew into Gunner's nostrils, and I rubbed the cocoa-colored gelding on his forehead, tracing the small white star, at which Gunner pinned his ears jealously. Plumber was much neater-looking than Gunner; his winter coat was fairly short and shiny, and he didn't tend to grow long hair under his jaw or on his fetlocks. Since he seemed to stay just as comfortable as Gunner during winter storms, I was at a loss to understand nature's ways on this issue. It seemed to me that the main result of all that excess shag was to make Gunner a lot harder to clean up.

Haltering both horses, I tied them to the fence and began the process of brushing the dried mud off their coats, combing their manes and tails, and picking out their feet. Lonny came walking down the driveway from his house while I was engaged in this activity, a wide smile on his face, ready to begin the day's fun.

He hitched his dually pickup truck to the four-horse stock trailer while I finished brushing my two horses, then we caught Burt and Pistol and I turned Plumber back out into his corral. The colt was still slightly off in his right front, the result of an injury that had been the reason I acquired him, and I didn't mean to start riding him until he was completely sound.

Gunner we loaded in the trailer, along with Burt and Pistol, and after a quick double-check of the hitch and door latch to make sure both were safely closed, I lifted Blue into the cab of Lonny's truck and we were off.

The mixed weather of the day before had cleared; the sky was deep winter blue, new grass brilliantly green on the hills. I smiled at the dazzle of wild mustard in full bloom in an old apple orchard—the almost unnaturally vivid fluorescent yellow startling against the dark gray skeleton shapes of the trunks.

As we neared Salinas, the round hills along Highway 101 slowly flattened into the broad plain of the Salinas River Valley. Lonny made the right turn onto Martinez Road, headed for Freddy's arena. Fifteen minutes later we pulled into the dirt entry road.

Trucks and trailers were parked randomly in the flat field next to the roping arena, with ropers and their horses visible everywhere. The arena itself, with its old much-repaired wooden fences weathered to silver gray, surrounded on three sides by an amphitheater of green hills, seemed even more historically colorful than usual this sunny morning.

Freddy waved a friendly hand at me as I got out of the truck, and I waved back. In some ways, Freddy himself was almost a personification of California history.

Freddy was Freddy Martinez, seventy years young; he'd been running a roping in this arena on the outskirts of Salinas for fifty of those seventy years. Freddy often said he was married to the arena (giving the exact number of years at the time); like most of Freddy's pronouncements, it was something you tended to hear expressed frequently and loudly.

He was loading cattle into the chute now, a short, stocky olive-skinned man with a look of latent power despite his age. His voice, a cheerful bellow, rose at regular intervals, scolding his help, pushing the cattle, calling to the arriving ropers. Doing what he'd been doing for generations. Freddy, the living legend.

As Jack Hollister had been, I thought suddenly, the image of Jack dousing my good spirits like a bucket of ice water. Jack, who had been murdered, shot through the head, should have been here this morning, warming up his horse in the sunshine, talking to his friends. My eyes sought and found Bronc, riding Willy in the center of a knot of people, all of them on horseback, walking slowly around the arena. Everyone seemed to be talking at Bronc, who, uncharacteristically, looked quiet. People saying they were sorry about Jack, I thought, wanting to know what had happened, speculating on who, how.

Watching Bronc pace silently around the arena, I was struck by the fact that he looked very alone. Jack would normally have been riding next to him, laughing and telling stories in that courtly way he had, all noblesse oblige, the perfect contrast and complement to Bronc's noisy hilarity.

Where was Trav, I wondered suddenly, and then spotted him on the other side of the arena, talking with a group of kids. Well, men in their twenties. Though I wasn't much older than these guys, they always seemed like kids to me—a certain frisky, puppyish quality in their behavior lending itself to that impression. But why wasn't Trav with Bronc? The thought had barely crossed my mind when it was followed by another. Bronc had seemed strangely reticent about Trav yesterday. Was something wrong between them? Maybe I could talk to Trav.

But not now. Lonny was unloading the horses and tying them to the trailer; it was time to get to work. I helped him saddle; as soon as we were done he swung up on Gunner. At five years of age, Gunner was still pretty green as a rope horse and it fell to Lonny, as the more experienced roper, to do the training. I was barely able to manage riding my horse and roping a cow at the same time; training a young horse simultaneously would have been way beyond me.

Getting Blue out of the cab, I walked him for a while, then put him in the horse trailer where he'd have more space and ventilation. After I was sure he was comfortable I climbed on Burt and rode into the arena.

Almost immediately I was absorbed into the friendly bustle

of the ropers—people saying hi, horses nickering to other horses, over all Freddy's raucous voice admonishing one John Porter to watch where he left his car parked all night, folks would notice. Everyone in the arena heard; I suspected people two miles away in downtown Salinas might have heard, too. Freddy's voice was almost as famous as he was; he'd never installed a loudspeaker at his arena and none was necessary.

Smiling at the banter, I took in the day and the crowd of horses and people and my heart lifted. Warm winter sunshine filled the south-facing bowl of hills that ringed the arena; grass glowed green on every rounded curve. Even the air smelled green. I felt as if someone had rolled spring into a ball and tossed it at me, saying "catch."

Reaching down to pat Burt's neck in the only expression of gratitude I could come up with, I grinned when he pinned his ears crossly—a characteristic response. Burt was a grouch. Tough-minded and irascible, he walked away when a human approached to catch him, humped his back when the cinch was pulled tight, and pinned his ears ferociously when he was touched or even spoken to. It was all bluff, though. Burt was as willing and pleasant a horse to ride as could be imagined (once one warmed the hump out of his back with some easy walking and trotting). He'd taught me to rope virtually single-handedly, ignoring my clumsy signals or lack thereof, and doing his job perfectly over and over again. It was due to him that I'd developed the confidence to begin competing.

I kicked him up into an easy lope and watched Lonny loping Gunner. In contrast to Burt's relaxed demeanor, Gunner was all eyes and ears, spooking constantly at things that struck him as "horse eaters." I wasn't surprised; this was only Gunner's fourth trip to a real roping arena; all his previous experience had been in Lonny's practice pen at home. On top of which, Gunner had a spooky streak—a strong inclination to jump first and ask questions later.

As I watched, Tommy Branco tossed his rope playfully at Gunner's heels, then laughed as the colt scooted forward abruptly. Lonny laughed, too, sitting squarely in the middle of the saddle, not even bothering to pick up the reins. That, I reflected, was one of Lonny's great advantages on a horse. His confidence gave his horses confidence.

Freddy was bellowing at us again, ordering the ropers out of the arena; it was time for the roping to begin. Compliantly the cowboys filed out; we were all well broke to Freddy's commands. As I guided Burt through the gate, I was struck by the fact that the crowd around me, though equally horsy, was a very different group from yesterday's endurance riders.

Mostly male as opposed to mostly female, clad exclusively in blue jeans, the ropers had a rough-edged look that was somehow evocative of ranches, though baseball caps were as prevalent as cowboy hats, tennis shoes were almost as common as boots, and no pretense was made, either by men or women, of the fringed and beaded look seen line dancing at Western bars. The horses, too, were horses of "another color"; while Rebby had been the lone representative Quarter Horse in a herd of Arabs, team-roping horses were predominantly of Quarter Horse breeding, and most were big and stout. All in all, there was an essential frontier spirit in the friendly group that jostled around me this morning; I could picture these ropers signing up to cross the prairie with a herd of longhorns.

"We're entered. Number thirty-one." Lonny gave me a wide smile as he rode up beside me and I nodded, feeling my heart start to pound nervously.

Par for the course. I'd only started competing at team roping a few months ago, and I always had a mild attack of nerves before I rode into the box. Turning Burt away, I walked over and parked him behind the chute, where I could watch the roping and rehearse what I needed to do.

Freddy was calling the teams out now; from my vantage point behind the chute I watched team number one, which turned out to be Travis and Bronc. They couldn't be too upset with each other, then. Trav was backing the sorrel mare he rode into the corner of the header's box. His face looked very young as he signaled with a short jerk of his chin and Freddy flipped the lever that opened the gate and released the steer.

In a split second all the poised, quiet tension of the moment erupted into violent motion. The steer leaped out the open gate of the chute and Trav's mare burst out after him, with Bronc on the heeler's side following their lead. Off they went down the arena, the steer running as fast as he could, both horses in hot pursuit.

Trav caught up to the steer about halfway to the end and roped it cleanly around the horns. Dallying his rope around the saddle horn, he turned his horse off and began to pull the steer. Bronc came in for the heel shot, Willy pinning his ears as he closed in.

Bronc threw his rope, the open loop landing neatly in front of the steer's back legs. Pulled by the head horse, the steer landed in the loop and Bronc jerked his arm back, tightening the noose. Another second and the ropes came tight; the flagger dropped the flag to record time.

Ten seconds—a respectable run. I hoped I could do as well. Hell, I hoped I could just manage to turn my steer.

Swallowing hard, I turned Burt away and began to walk him around the dirt parking lot, keeping him loose. At twelve years, Burt was old enough and had enough miles on him that his hocks tended to get stiff if he stood still too long. Thus I always tried to get him warmed up before we made a run.

Team roping moves quickly. In just a few minutes, it seemed, Freddy was on number twenty-seven. Soon it would be my turn.

I loped Burt up and down the sandy parking lot and stopped him abruptly. He checked easily in response to my cue, and I walked him out, confident he would respond to me in the course of the run. Burt was about as foolproof as a rope horse could get.

Freddy called out number thirty-one and I rode Burt through the little gate in the side of the header's box and backed him into the corner. My heart was pounding; I could feel Burt's heart pounding between my legs.

I glanced over to the heeler's box to see Lonny sitting at his ease on Gunner, who was dancing in nervous agitation. Lonny gave me a wide, encouraging smile.

Shifting my attention to the chute I fixed my eyes on the steer, a red and white spotted longhorn. Rule number one of team roping: Never take your eyes off the steer.

A longhorn—that probably meant speed. Gearing myself to drive Burt hard, I took a deep breath, steadied my hand on the reins, and nodded. With a clang, Freddy's hand dropped, the gate flew open, and the red and white steer leapt out.

Giving Burt his head, I sent him in pursuit, and the whole world vanished in a blur of speed and power. All I could feel was the horse running, all I could see was the steer, his horns bobbing to the rhythm of his driving strides. Inexorably Burt was closing the gap. We drew closer, closer.

I swung my rope with as much force as I knew how, trying to feel the weight of it, as I had been taught. We were on the steer now, Burt "rating" over the steer's left hip like the reliable horse he was, giving me a shot.

I swung the rope one more time, measuring distances with my eye, and threw it, letting my body take over, doing it on automatic pilot. My mind registered that the loop went on and I pulled it tight, taking the slack out.

Now dally the rope around the saddle horn, the dangerous part, the part where ropers lose fingers. Again my body made the moves cleanly on automatic pilot, Burt staying close to the steer, giving me the time I needed to dally safely.

Dallies secure, I reined him off to the left, feeling him gather himself to pull as he picked up the weight of the steer and began to tow him. I looked back over my shoulder, watching the steer. Rule number two, three, and four of team roping: Never take your eye off the steer.

The red and white longhorn made a particularly high leap on the end of the rope and Lonny delivered his loop neatly, snagging the steer's two hind feet while they were in the air. Gunner stopped hard, bringing the heel rope tight, and I whirled Burt around to face them. Time.

Eleven and a half seconds, not bad for a beginner. I smiled as Lonny and I put slack in our ropes to let the longhorn up. He scrambled to his feet and trotted off unconcernedly; he'd been roped plenty of times before.

Lonny looked pleased and patted Gunner's neck. "The colt did real good," he told me.

"That's great. I didn't really get to see much of him. I was too busy keeping my end under control."

"You done good." Lonny gave me a wide grin as we rode back up the arena.

A familiar voice hollered at me in raucous tones from the fence. "Sweetheart, any time you want a new partner, you just let me know."

Bronc. At least he wasn't feeling too bad to tease. I smiled in his direction and was rewarded by a wolfish baring of the teeth. Good sign.

I got a few congratulatory comments from the other ropers and stood behind the chutes for a minute, basking in the warmth and relief of a job well done. Then it was time to prepare myself for the next steer.

Freddy's jackpots were "three steers" and "progressive after one," which meant that if you roped your first steer you got a second one, and if your time was good on these two steers you got a "high-team run" on the third steer. Quickest time on three steers won the roping.

I started moving Burt around at the walk, then the trot. Not too long until we would be up again.

My heart did its pounding-in-the-chest routine once more as I backed into the header's box for my second run. The steer in the chute was black and white and had the look of a Holstein cross. Slow, I thought. Probably slow. Freddy grinned at me as I met his eyes. "Good one, sweetheart. Just for you."

I nodded my head, Freddy opened the gate, the black and

white steer galloped out. Giving Burt his head, I dashed after him. The steer was slow all right, but he was also crooked. Just as we caught up to him, he cut left, virtually disappearing under Burt's neck.

On another horse I might have pulled up, since the wreck that ensues when the head horse stumbles over a steer and goes down is one of my worst nightmares, but Burt was that rare and unique individual—a horse that virtually won't fall. I could feel him bounce off the steer's back end, then lift himself up, avoid tangling his feet, and move over to the left, showing me the steer once more. I had a shot. I threw.

Miraculously, or so it seemed to me at the moment, the loop settled on the steer's horns. I pulled it tight, dallied, and turned Burt. He towed the animal off easily, and I could see Lonny and Gunner come in behind it. Lonny took a quick shot, the ropes came tight, and the flagger dropped the flag.

Eight point nine seconds—the quickest run I'd made to date. I felt a wide grin breaking out on my face as I turned to Lonny. He was grinning back. "That worked."

"Yeah," I said, "it did."

"We'll be high team out," he added. "Probably."

Uh-oh. My high spirits took a quick dive. I'd never been high team before. Nerves would likely destroy me. If you let them, I told myself. Only if you let them.

But I could already feel the fist clenching itself inside my gut. Only about half a dozen more teams left to run and high teams would be called. At Freddy's, high teams were run in order; the fastest time on two steers went first, next fastest second and so on, until there were no more teams who had a legitimate chance. Legitimate chance in this case translated into 6.5 seconds, which was the fastest time ever recorded at Freddy's. If a team could place with a 6.5 run, they were allowed to take a shot at it.

I, on the other hand, was highly unlikely to rope a steer in anywhere close to six seconds. In fact, I thought a little desperately, I was pretty unlikely to catch and turn three in a row.

That was no way to think. I knew how to do this. Quit worrying, I told myself. Empty your mind. Free your body up to do the job it knows how to do.

Obediently, I turned Burt away from the chutes and began to walk him around. I swung my rope, loosening my muscles, and reminded myself firmly that it was just another steer. You can rope him or not rope him, it's not the end of the world, Gail.

Almost immediately, it seemed, I heard Freddy's raucous voice calling high teams. "First out is gonna be Gail McCarthy and Lonny Peterson with twenty point four."

Here we go. I was conscious of friendly smiles and encouraging looks coming my way as I walked toward the box. Burt's ears, red with black tips, grew stiff with tension as I maneuvered him into the back corner. Like all rope horses, he knew what was coming.

Keeping a firm hand on the reins, I steadied him as I looked at the steer. He was white, a Charlais cross. What that meant, God only knew. Charlais were notoriously unpredictable. He might run hard, might be crooked, might even stop in front of me.

What the hell. I increased the pressure on the reins slightly, tucked my rope under my arm, and met Freddy's eyes. Blanking every thought out of my mind, I nodded for the steer.

The gate clanged open; the white steer jumped forward. I released Burt, who sprang forward after him like a rocket off its pad. The steer ran hard—I could feel Burt driving, accelerating; I urged him with my body and he closed the gap in a sudden spurt.

I swung the rope, feeling the weight of it, focusing on the steer and throwing out of the swing. The loop curled crisply around the horns, I pulled the slack without fumbling, dallied, and let Burt tow the steer off, a tide of relief washing over me like a wave.

I'd done it, I'd caught and turned the steer. I was barely aware of Lonny and Gunner coming in for the heel shot, didn't see where Lonny's loop went. I saw the rope come tight and whirled Burt around to face as the flagger dropped the flag. Only then did I notice Lonny's sheepish expression. He'd caught one of the steer's legs rather than two—an automatic extra five seconds would be added to our time.

"Sorry, Gail," he said as we put slack in the ropes so the steer could get up. "I didn't get the loop all the way under him."

"That's okay," I told him, still feeling the glow of happiness from the awareness that I'd got it done. I'd competed under pressure and come through. At the moment, I didn't really care if we placed or not.

Lonny, on the other hand, shook his head in frustration. "Damn. I had a perfect shot, too. This colt worked like a champ." He patted Gunner's neck with one hand, and I looked at my blaze-faced bay horse and smiled with all the pride of a mother whose kid has won first prize at the science fair.

Our time was announced as 15.5, which, on top of 20.4 made us 35.9 on three steers. Respectable, but hardly quick.

I rode Burt over near the chutes to sit next to Lonny and Gunner and watch the other high teams go. Part of me wanted them all to miss, so that we could win the pot. The less than admirable part of me. I told myself that they all wanted and perhaps needed to win as much as I did and tried to watch the competition with a detached eye.

Four teams had already run; everyone had missed or legged their steers. We were still winning as I watched Katie Garcia ride her gray gelding, Clyde, toward the header's box. Katie was a good roper, far more proficient than I was; she'd been raised in a roping family and had started competing in her early teens. She was also a friendly, outgoing person who had given me several helpful tips when I first started and was always supportive. I liked her a great deal, and I especially liked her horse.

Clyde was one of those special horses who took your heart. He tried hard, had a kind eye, did his best every run, within his limitations. His big suitcase of a head didn't have any classic eye appeal, and his bulky body and thick bones made him slower than was desirable for a head horse, but he was a good one, nonetheless.

I was watching him now, thinking what a nice horse he was and that I wouldn't mind so much if Katie was the one to beat me, when suddenly things started to go wrong.

It happened, as most accidents do, so quickly that it was virtually unpreventable. One minute Katie was urging Clyde into the header's box, the big gray gelding dancing a little and fretting. Like many rope horses, he often had a mild attack of jitters when he was about to perform. For no particular reason he backed up three or four strides, and his rear end bumped the front of the old water truck Freddy had parked near the chutes.

One moment he was backing and tossing his head, the next his leg was caught. Against all likelihood his right hind leg, in a backward reaching stride, had slid into the gap between the front bumper and the body of the truck. Clyde jerked his leg upward sharply in an attempt to free it, and succeeded only in wedging his fetlock immovably. Before any of us realized precisely what had happened, Katie was clinging to the horse's neck as he lunged and struggled to get loose, her face both frightened and confused.

"He's caught in the truck," someone yelled.

"Get off of him," came from another quarter.

Katie bailed awkwardly off and grabbed the reins. I could hear Lonny's voice next to me, low and rough with emotion. "He's going to tear his foot right off."

Without thinking, I jumped off Burt and moved quickly toward the struggling Clyde. "Whoa now," I said as I put a hand firmly on the lurching gray rump and leaned my shoulder into his flank, trying to force him to hold still. Running my hand down toward his hock, I took the pose of a shoer holding up a hind foot. I put all my muscles and my will into holding him there.

To my relief, I could feel Clyde stop struggling. He stood on three legs, his right hind fetlock pinched in the vise of the bumper, my shoulder pressed against his quivering flank. Katie was holding his head and talking to him. Despite the fact that I could see bright red blood staining his gray ankle, he wasn't moving, at least for the moment.

Several more people converged in our direction when Freddy's bellow froze everyone in place. "Don't scare him," he shouted in the voice that had become famous all over California. "Stand back. Gail there is enough."

In Freddy's hands was a crowbar; where he'd gotten it or how he'd managed to produce it so quickly, I had no idea. Quietly he moved up to Clyde, patting his shoulder as he approached the bumper where the horse's leg was caught.

Freddy got the crowbar under the bumper and began prying carefully. Stay quiet, Clyde, I pleaded silently as I pressed steadily against his flank.

It seemed to take forever. I could see the muscles under Freddy's shirt strain. That thick, stout body with its heavy ham-like arms worked against the metal, struggling to get the bumper loose. For long minutes Freddy looked anything but old as he slowly pried the bumper away from the fender, the metal giving up with a long rending screech.

Leaning hard against Clyde's flank to steady him, I reached a hand gently down the horse's trapped leg and pulled it free as Freddy's crowbar inexorably widened the gap between fender and bumper. Clyde held his leg up for a second, trembling, as blood dripped off of it, then set the foot gingerly down on the ground and stood. I breathed a deep sigh of relief. Clyde was able to bear weight on his leg.

"Do you want me to have a look at it?" I asked Katie.

"Please." Katie's face was calm, as was her voice, but I could see tears in her eyes. She was petting Clyde's neck gently, reflexively, over and over.

"I'll get my emergency kit and be right back."

The emergency kit was in the tack box of the horse trailer. A small, waterproof chest, it contained tranquilizers, painkillers, needles and syringes, antibiotics, bandaging materials, thermometer, stethoscope, and wound dressing. At the very bottom was a kill shot, loaded and waiting. Thank God it wasn't needed now. Packing the whole chest back to where Clyde was standing, I gave him a shot of butazone in the jugular vein—to reduce the pain and keep inflammation at a minimum—then washed the wound, which was less severe than it appeared, stitched it, and applied a pressure wrap. Giving Katie a bottle of antibiotics and some bute pills, I told her, "Keep him on these for five days; the dosages are written on the bottles. You'll need to rewrap this every other day at first. Then after a week, every third day. Two weeks from now, let me or your regular vet have a look—the stitches can probably come out then."

"Okay." Katie nodded and took the stuff. She was still rubbing Clyde's neck. "Thanks, Gail."

I smiled and rubbed the horse's neck, too. "I think he'll be all right."

"I sure hope so."

Katie led Clyde off toward her trailer. He limped, but he could walk. I felt an immeasurable relief and gratitude, and said a small prayer of thanks.

Lonny tapped me on the shoulder and I turned. "He gonna be okay?" Lonny's eyes were concerned.

"I think so."

"That's good." He handed me a hundred-dollar bill. "Your share. We won. It paid two hundred dollars."

"It did?" For a moment I was confused. I'd forgotten all about the competition, didn't realize that the rest of the high teams had been taking their turns as I was working on Clyde. I hadn't even heard Freddy bellowing out the winners. Under the circumstances the money seemed anticlimactic.

But still, my first win. Smiling at Lonny, I tried to conjure up a congratulatory attitude and felt myself grabbed and hugged from behind. Lonny's face registered only amusement; before I could react further I heard Bronc's rough voice in my ear. "Honey, I could use a roping partner like you. You bring in the money and you could stitch up my old pony when he gets hurt. You ready to trade old Lonny in on a better model?"

Lonny howled with laughter at that. "At least you can't say younger, Bronc."

Turning, I gave Bronc a quick hug.

"Anytime," he chuckled. "Anytime."

Looking at Lonny, I said, "I'll unsaddle Gunner, if you're done with him."

"Thanks." Lonny was already getting on Pistol. "Don't you want to rope anymore?" he asked me.

"I don't think so. I've had enough action for one day. I think I'll quit while I'm ahead."

Lonny barely heard me; he was already riding away. His mind was focused on competing and anything that didn't pertain to that he tended to ignore.

This was fine with me. I untied Gunner and climbed on him, scanning the crowd. What I was planning to do next was something Lonny definitely wouldn't have approved of. I was going to corner Trav and have a talk.

ELEVEN

Cornering Trav turned out to be easy. I simply rode up to him where he sat on his little sorrel mare, watching the roping.

Travis looked as he always did, a tall, slender kid with an unremarkable face—brown eyes and hair, fair skin, a strong chin—wearing Wrangler jeans and tennis shoes with spurs, a T-shirt that said No Fear, and a lime green baseball cap. He sat on the mare with his usual relaxed grace—the quiet, understated poise of the natural horseman. Only the expression on his face was different. Travis, normally exuberantly friendly, looked somber.

I was reminded suddenly of all the talk—that Travis was really Jack's son, the result of one of his many extramarital flings. That was why he'd hired Trav and let him live on the ranch, given him a horse and taken him roping—so people said. Just who had told me this? I tried to remember and couldn't. It was talk—stories that had clung to Travis for as long as I'd known him.

Which was for two or three years, more or less. I'd met him on one of my first calls out to the Hollister Ranch; Jack and Bronc had both been out of town and Travis had had a colicked horse. I could still remember my first impression of Trav—young, friendly, worried, anxious to do right by the horse, eager to comprehend my instructions. Unlike a good many men in their twenties, Travis wasn't on any kind of a macho trip. Fortunately, the horse had made a complete recovery and, ever since, Travis and I had been friendly. Not friends, exactly—I knew nothing of his personal life, and he knew as little of mine. But we chatted amiably together when we saw each other, mostly about horses, which was, of course, what we had in common, and my initial impression had only been confirmed. Travis was a genuinely nice, easygoing kid.

"I'm sorry about Jack," I said to him.

His eyes shifted to my face and then back to the roping. "Me too." There was a long moment of uncharacteristic silence. Finally he said, "I heard you were up there when it happened." The words seem to come out reluctantly, and he kept his eyes on the activity in the arena.

"Yeah," I agreed. "A friend of mine was out with him the night he was killed."

Travis looked at me briefly. "Do the cops suspect her?"

"I don't think so."

More uncomfortable silence.

"What will you do now?" I asked him at last.

"Stay on the ranch and work for Bronc." There was some emotion in his voice, something I couldn't place.

"I hear Jack left the ranch to be part of the state park."

"Yep." Travis didn't seem curious as to how I had heard it. "Bronc and I get to live there, just like we are, and take care of it. It's in Jack's will."

"That's good."

Travis still stared almost fixedly at the team roping, his usual lighthearted, youthful demeanor completely absent. In his stern expression was a faint resemblance to Jack's typical firm-jawed visage and I was reminded yet again of the talk that Trav was really Jack's son. And yet Bronc had said Jack was sterile.

Deciding these were hardly questions I could ask Travis, I said, I hoped lightly, "The cops spent two days questioning me up in Tahoe. Have you been through that, too?"

"Oh yeah. They came out and grilled me and Bronc. Don't

make no difference, though. Bronc and I can give each other alibis." Trav said this firmly, then jerked his chin toward the chute. "I'm up in a minute."

With the words, he wheeled the mare and trotted off, looking, I thought, relieved to be rid of me. Well, what did I expect? These were probably the last things he wanted to think or talk about. Still, it was odd the way he had volunteered that Bronc and he could alibi each other. Living on the same ranch as they did, it would be easy to see why this would be the case, but why was he so quick to tell me?

And why so unfriendly? His unnatural reticence could be the way he dealt with grief, but somehow it had seemed more than that. Almost hostile. I wondered suddenly if Travis might believe Joanna had killed Jack and I was covering for her.

Riding Gunner back to Lonny's trailer, I unsaddled him and brushed him, then took Blue for a slow walk. After that I drank a beer with a couple of friendly ropers while I watched Lonny and Bronc win the third pot of the day. Bronc managed to heel all three steers neatly by two feet to beat a good seventy teams, despite the fact that he was the oldest roper in the arena. I cheered them on happily, forgetting, for the moment, Jack's murder, and simply enjoying the sunny day and the ambiance.

It wasn't until the roping was over and we were unsaddling Burt and Pistol, that trouble returned. It came in the form of a battered blue pickup that pulled in the front gate and rolled to a stop in the parking lot, not far from our rig. A woman got out and leaned on the fender, smoking a cigarette with jerky, abrupt motions. Tara Hollister.

I couldn't stand Tara Hollister. Everything from her too obviously dyed blond hair to her hard-faced, tough-girl attitude, to her skintight, overly sexy clothes grated on my nerves, but nothing so much as the idea that she posed as a horse trainer. Despite the fact that to even a moderately knowledgeable eye she was not a very good hand with a horse, she had managed to convince a few even more ignorant folks of her abilities, and always seemed to have two or three horses "in training."

I had a very low tolerance for the sound of Tara's deep, somewhat harsh voice pontificating along the lines of "that son-of-a-bitch just needs a shorter tiedown and a good whack alongside the head, and he'd be all right in the box." Mostly it was bullshit, and I guess I've got a low bullshit tolerance. But more than that, I thought Tara was often downright cruel, and I don't put up with cruelty at all.

"There's Tara," Lonny said, following my line of sight to the figure beside the truck. "You gonna go over there and question her?"

He was half playful, half serious; I'd already considered doing just that.

"No," I said finally, "I'd better not."

"Why not?"

"Because I'm a witness in that trial she's involved in, and I'm afraid she'll ask me questions about that. It's tomorrow," I added, mostly to myself.

"Trial?" Lonny said blankly.

"Remember? The night she rode that sorrel gelding to death? Well, she's suing the former owner. You know."

"Oh yeah." Lonny's face was rueful. "I forgot about that."

I wasn't surprised. Lonny had a selective memory to go with his optimistic attitude; he tended to remember only those things that were pleasant or directly relevant to what he needed to do. The unpleasant and unnecessary details of life were neatly forgotten. And Tara's lawsuit, a matter of small claims court, was just such a sorry transaction. I didn't like to think about it either, as the whole thing seemed both sad, ridiculous, and awkward.

"You ready to go?" Lonny grinned at me. His mind had clearly switched back to the enjoyable ending of a typical roping day—a drink, dinner, and a roll in the hay.

"I guess so." My mind was elsewhere, but I obediently helped him load the three horses in the trailer and was putting Blue in the truck when I heard voices raised in the unequivocal tones of a major argument. Everyone in the arena heard; conversations and motion came to a fascinated stop as the whole place craned its attention on Tara Hollister and Bronc, who were shouting at each other over by his rig.

"That's my horse, you know damn well he is. He was born out of one of Jack's mares while I was married to Jack, and I'm taking him back." Tara's usually low voice was shrill with anger.

"Bullshit." Bronc spat on the ground at Tara's feet. "This horse is mine just like everything on that ranch is mine. And if you were a man, you ring-tailed bitch, I'd make you remember it."

He turned and led Willy toward the rear of the trailer, every muscle of his body hard. Tara raised her arms, hands curled into claws, and sprang on his back, her fingernails gouging at his face. Lips pulled tight over her teeth, she screeched, "You think so, you motherfucker? Try it."

There was a collective gasp. Thrown punches were not unknown at roping arenas, and I had witnessed two twentyish women clawing at each other in precisely this way a month ago, over a blond kid I would have said was not worth the trouble. But the spectacle of a woman attacking a man of Bronc's age seemed absurdly shocking.

Bronc was doubled over, Tara clinging to his back, clawing and kicking as his arms sought a purchase on her body, angry ejaculations shooting from his mouth. Tara, for her part, was still screeching, though I couldn't make out words anymore.

By this time people nearby had recovered from their surprise at the sight, and two youngish ropers jumped into the melee and grabbed Tara, pulling her off Bronc. She was still shouting insults and made some attempt to claw at the men holding her, at which one of them shook her lightly with a muttered "Calm down."

Bronc, for his part, wiped the blood from a wicked-looking scratch on his cheek, and turned to take Willy's reins from Trav, who had caught the startled horse. He stared at Tara, being held by her elbows, and then spat again. "You'll have this horse over my dead body, you little murdering bitch."

He led Willy into the stock trailer, loaded Trav's mare behind him, tied the two horses and latched the door, then walked around and got in his pickup. Trav climbed in the passenger side quickly. Starting the engine, Bronc said a brief "Thanks" to the two men who were still holding Tara, and pulled out of the parking lot. Only when his rig disappeared down Martinez Road did Tara's captors release her.

Rubbing her elbows, she glared at them malevolently, then climbed into her own truck and proceeded to skid out of the parking lot in an adolescent display of bad temper. The whole crowd watched her departure, eyes wide. This was definitely the stuff of which gossip was made.

"Whew." Lonny had started his truck and was nosing it out of the parking lot at a considerably more sedate pace. Ignoring the little knots of chatting, gesticulating ropers gathered by their rigs, he bumped on down the drive toward the road. Lonny wasn't much of a gossiper.

Left to myself, I might have stayed to talk, but my motives, I assured myself, were more professional than mere curiosity. If anyone had ever looked like a creature who could murder out of rage, Tara's contorted face had looked it this afternoon.

"How in the world could he have married her?" I said out loud.

Lonny had no trouble understanding what I meant. He shook his head, then smiled deprecatingly. I looked at him curiously; his expression was almost sheepish.

"What are you thinking?" I demanded.

"I'm almost embarrassed to say it."

"Come on."

He sighed. "Jack was in his fifties. Just a little older than I am." He glanced in my direction. "Tara's what, midthirties? And whatever else you can say about her, she's got a good body. She makes sure you notice." He gave a brief laugh.

"You're saying he married her just to get in the pants of a youngish, decent-looking woman? That he was so stupid, or going through such a midlife crisis that he didn't look beyond that? That's hard to believe."

I thought about Jack as I had known him—a handsome, wealthy man, a confirmed flirt certainly, but not obnoxiously so. I'd seen no hint of desperation in his eyes. And there would have been no reason for it. Plenty of women would have been willing to take on Jack Hollister.

"Why?" I asked Lonny. "Why would you think that?"

Lonny didn't answer, but looked more sheepish than ever.

Watching his profile as he drove, the answer dawned on me by degrees. "Is that what you feel about me?"

His hesitation was its own answer. "Of course not," was what he eventually said. "But I've wondered, sometimes, if there wasn't an element of that. It bothers me a little."

We were both silent. Lonny was fourteen years older than me, hardly the gap of the century. But it was a gap, nonetheless, and there were times when I noticed how youthful I appeared next to him. Normally this was pleasant, but there were moments when it struck me as mildly incongruous. After all, the farcical elements of a May/December romance were as old as human history.

"So," I said slowly, "you're saying that Jack, and maybe you, were, shall we say, thinking with your peckers when you got involved with younger women."

Lonny laughed. "I hope it's not that simple. But there's an element of that in most men. Jack had a lot of it, I think."

I chewed on that awhile. I had to admit, the subject was becoming a lot more personal, and I was perhaps more interested in Lonny's motivations than Jack's. Eventually, though, I dragged my mind off my own feelings and tried to analyze what Jack's motivation for marrying Tara might have to do with his subsequent murder.

"So let's say Jack married her because she was relatively young and good-looking and could ride a horse. An ornament to his manhood, shall we say, something he could take to the roping arenas and be all puffed up about. Maybe she was good in bed, even. But he rapidly grows disenchanted, and starts running around on her, which we all know he did. So Tara demands a divorce and a bunch of money and, we suppose, gets it. So where'd the money go, anyway—she doesn't look rich."

Lonny seemed relieved to be off the subject of his own motivation and back on Jack and, for once, entered into the spirit of investigation with some enthusiasm. "She did for a while. This was before you started to go roping. Right after Tara broke up with Jack she was driving a rig that must have cost a quarter of a million and buying horses hand over fist. She bought a pretty fancy place, too, or so I heard. But over the last couple of years it's all disappeared."

I nodded. I'd heard this.

"As to where it went," Lonny looked mildly disgusted, "I don't know this, but I've been told she uses drugs."

He said it as if it were a contaminated subject, which to a man of his age and stamp, it was. I felt less strongly about it, though those few people I'd known who were habitual users of cocaine or speed had not been likable characters. And, it struck me suddenly, the taut, high-strung, irritably nervous energy they'd sometimes displayed seemed to fit Tara's apparently irrational attack on Bronc. Could some sort of drug-induced frenzy have prompted her to murder Jack? That and the idea she'd inherit?

"Drugs can run through your money," I commented.

Lonny said nothing, but I knew he and I were both thinking of a well-to-do roper we both knew who had started indulging in cocaine several years ago. He'd managed to relieve himself of a successful tractor dealership, several hundred acres of inherited farm land and a paid-off family ranch in remarkably short order and was currently living in a battered travel trailer on an old friend's property without a nickel to his name. If he could manage it, so could Tara.

All right, I said to myself, she could have run through the money on fast living and wanted more, Bronc said she knew the terms of the will, drugs could have made her irrational enough to kill, but was she in Tahoe that night? Of course, that didn't necessarily mean anything. She could have promised to split her inheritance with whoever did the dirty work for her. But Bronc had called her a "murdering bitch." And he had been suddenly silent the other night when I had asked him if he thought Tara killed Jack. What did Bronc know?

And there was something else. I turned back to Lonny. "That whole fight she just had with Bronc was over Willy. Do you know anything about that?"

"Not really. I did hear her get into it with Bronc before about that horse. She seems to think she has some right to him."

Now how did that connect? I suddenly felt like laughing. Was I about to construct a scenario in which Tara murdered Jack in order to get Willy away from Bronc?

Sensing my change of mood, Lonny reached across the seat and took my hand. "What do you say we forget all this stuff and go have a nice dinner at the Harbor Inn?"

The Harbor Inn. I smiled at the thought. A spectacular view of the old boat harbor at Moss Landing, complete with ancient piers, sea otters, pelicans, and herons, not to mention equally spectacular fresh fish to eat. And I would, of course, be seeing Tara the next morning, like it or not. Time enough to think about her then.

"You're saying that if I quit worrying about this murder for tonight you'll take me to dinner at the Harbor Inn?"

"And show you a good time, too." Lonny's grin was full of promise.

"You're on."

TWELVE

At nine o'clock the next morning I was pacing the cold halls of the county building, searching for small claims court. It wasn't, fortunately, a place I was familiar with, and I was several minutes late as I slipped in the door and found a spot in a back pew. The room was fairly full of people, most of whom I didn't recognize, but a few were glaringly familiar.

Tara, of course, I spotted at once, looking incongruous in a boldly patterned, clingy rayon dress. She was flanked by a couple of young, rough-looking ropers that I recognized by face though not by name. They were fringe hangers-on in the roping world, usually too broke to own a horse or come up with the entry money, but often standing on the sidelines, beer in hand.

In another corner, with a scowl on his face, was a heavyset middle-aged man named Harvey Reynolds, the defendant. A sometime roper of limited capabilities, he had sold Tara the horse that had subsequently died. Harvey was surrounded by quite a group of people, several of them ropers who had been at Freddy's yesterday. This whole gang was chatting freely together, whispering loudly, and casting plenty of glares at Tara.

My own position here was somewhat ambiguous. I was the

vet Harvey had used when he'd owned the horse in question, a long-necked sorrel gelding he'd called JD. I was also, sadly, the vet who had been on call the night the horse had tied up and eventually died. Tara would no doubt have preferred Jim, my boss, but what she'd gotten was me, to our mutual dissatisfaction. In terms of the horse it hadn't made any difference; poor JD would have died no matter who had been treating him.

I was only glad I hadn't been there to see what led up to his demise; the story—which I'd heard recounted by several people—was bad enough at second hand. Apparently Tara had been training on the gelding that night in her usual fashion, jerking and janging on the bit when he wouldn't stand perfectly still in the box, and eventually resorting to whipping him over and over with the rope. Predictably, this made the horse worse, and Tara had run steer after steer on him in a futile effort to tire him into submission, despite the fact that he was clearly already exhausted.

According to universal consensus, she'd competed in the last pot with the horse wringing wet and starting to tie up. Several people had mentioned this to her, to no effect. She'd shrugged them off with a "He can run one more steer." In actual fact, she'd run six more, or tried to. By then the horse wasn't able to run.

I'd arrived several hours later at her place on an emergency call to find JD going into shock. I had him hauled down to the clinic and pumped fluids into him all night long, to no avail. By the next day he was in renal failure, and Tara was told the horse needed to be put down. I'd been so reluctant to deal with her that I'd asked Jim to make the call, and he'd reported that, as I'd expected, she'd blustered on and on about it being possibly my fault the horse was dying—which was palpably untrue, but par for the course with Tara.

After sufficient reflection, it seemed, she'd decided she would be unlikely to win a suit against me, and so had elected to sue the former owner of the horse, on the grounds that JD had a chronic problem with tying up, and Reynolds had failed to reveal this to her. Unfortunately for her, I'd been Harvey's vet the whole time he'd had the horse, and this simply wasn't true. JD had colicked once, which Tara had heard about through the roper's grapevine, and she was ignorant enough to suppose that the two problems were interchangeable. In actual fact they were quite different, both medically and practically speaking, not to mention that a whole arena of people could attest to the fact that the horse had tied up because Tara had overridden him, and he had almost certainly died because she didn't quit riding him when his muscles started to stiffen.

I'd been called into this ridiculous affair by both the principals. Tara seemed to expect that I would testify to the fact that the horse had died of tying up and that I had had to treat the horse for Harvey for the same condition. And Harvey, who knew good and well that the horse had colicked with him, not tied up, was expecting me to say so. Which I would. Tara wasn't going to like it. I just hoped she wouldn't resort to clawing my eyes out.

By the time the courtroom was called to order it was nine-thirty and I was already tapping my foot impatiently. I was virtually drumming my fingers and toes an hour later; every party had been called except ours. When the place was empty but for the little contingent of ropers, the bailiff finally called Tara Hollister versus Harvey Reynolds and we all trooped up to stand in front of the judge's bench. As plaintiff, it was left to Tara to begin.

She made a statement full of histrionics and pathos about how she had bought the horse in good faith, was devastated when it died, and aghast when she had heard from other ropers that the horse had tied up when Harvey owned him. She felt that Harvey should have disclosed this when he sold her the horse. There was lots more along these lines, all in a whiny pseudo-feminine tone that contrasted oddly with her gravelly cigarette smoker's voice.

I watched her as she talked, trying to see what Jack might have seen in her, trying to decide if she could be a murderer. Put

93

boldly like that it was hard to believe. Tara looked too tacky in her ugly dress, too dumb, too insubstantial somehow, to have planned and executed a murder. The idea that she had arranged for someone else to do it seemed to carry more weight.

As for what Jack had seen in her, I simply couldn't imagine. You're not a man, I reminded myself. But I had eyes. I noted the fit curves beneath the clingy rayon, the harsh country-western bar singer's sex appeal on her overly made-up face. What I couldn't understand is why the self-centered, low-IQ, no-heart expression in her eyes hadn't glared out at him as loudly as it did at me.

I was jerked away from my thoughts by the sound of my name, spoken in Tara's rough voice. "Dr. McCarthy treated my horse. She'll tell you what it died of."

Tara was addressing the judge, who looked inquiringly at the group of us. Obediently I stepped forward, identified myself, and began to describe the condition in which I'd found JD, and his subsequent deterioration. This took a while, as the judge was clearly unfamiliar with horses. A middle-aged Latino man with glasses and a bright expression, he asked several careful questions about the nature of azoturia, as tying up is technically called.

I explained that some horses did have a chronic problem with this, and that I did not know if this was true of JD. I mentally added that I was fairly sure it was not, and that the horse had simply been ridden to death, but I kept this to myself, no one having asked for my opinion.

Tara didn't ask me any questions; in fact, she wouldn't look at me, and the judge seemed to be done, so I backed up a step and merged into the group, half listening to the two rough-looking roping kids as Tara elicited from them a favorable description of her horse handling in general and the way she had treated JD on the night in question in particular. Nobody seemed inclined to speak up and tell the judge that neither of these guys would know proper treatment of a horse if they saw it. When, occasionally, they were not too broke to own a horse, both of them treated the unfortunate animal as an inexhaustible machine.

At long last Tara seemed to be done, and Harvey stepped forward to announce himself as the defendant; I breathed an inward sigh of relief. It was difficult to listen to so much bullshit and keep my mouth shut.

Harvey was obviously pissed as hell. He wasted no time on preliminary explanations, but simply said, "I would like to call Dr. Gail McCarthy."

Once again I stepped forward out of the group and faced the judge.

"Did you perform a vet check on JD when I bought him?" Harvey's tone was belligerent, but I knew the anger wasn't directed against me.

"Yes."

"At the time did you find anything wrong with the horse?"

"Nothing major. He had a few signs of arthritic changes."

"No sign he'd ever tied up before."

"Well no, but I don't think there's any way of determining that."

Harvey was like a bulldog with a hunk of German shepherd in his mouth. Tenacious. "But as far as you knew, or I knew, there was nothing of that sort wrong with the horse when I bought him."

"That's right."

"Did I ever call on you to treat the horse for being tied up while I had him?"

"No."

"Did I call on you to treat him at all?"

"Yes. Once. For colic."

"Not for tying up, for colic, right?"

"Right."

Here Harvey turned from me to the judge. "Your Honor, Dr. McCarthy, here, has been my vet the whole time I owned JD,

which was about two years. The horse colicked once and I had
him treated and he was fine. He never tied up in his life, as far
as I know."

The judge looked at me and asked for an explanation of the
difference between tying up and colic.

I tried not to be too technical. "Tying up, or azoturia, is a condition where the muscles produce an overabundance of lactic
acid, which they can't absorb. The symptoms include pain and
stiffness, a reluctance to move, and brown urine, as the kidneys
try to dispose of the excess acid. The cause is often too much
grain. A horse that is tying up should immediately be rested. On
no account should he be asked to move until his muscles relax."

I stopped for a breath. "Colic, on the other hand, is a term
covering any sort of upset in the digestive system. Colics can be
very mild and pass unnoticed, or they can be serious enough to
be fatal. A horse with colic will also show pain; however, that
is about the only real similarity. A colicky horse can often be
helped by light exercise, while a horse who has tied up should
remain still. People sometimes get confused about this; there's
a tendency to think you should walk a tied-up horse, but that's
wrong."

I stopped again. Shit. This judge didn't want to know what
to do when a horse tied up. I felt like I was rambling on to no
point in my efforts to make azoturia and colic plain to a non-
horseman.

"So there is no connection between the two conditions?" The
judge had obviously grasped the main idea.

"No, none at all."

"You may go on, Mr. Reynolds."

Harvey went on. And on and on. He called several people to
describe the way in which Tara had overridden the horse that
night, after which I was recalled to pronounce on whether such
overriding could produce a fatal case of azoturia. Naturally I
had to admit that it could. I could feel Tara's eyes slicing into
the back of my neck as I spoke.

Harvey called a good many more people; the clock on the wall said noon by the time he was done. I was feeling both impatient and annoyed when the judge asked to speak with me one more time.

"In your opinion, Dr. McCarthy, this horse could have died as a result of being fed a large amount of grain on a daily basis and being ridden to excess on the night in question, even if the horse did not have a prior history of"—the judge hesitated—"tying up?"

"That's right." I snapped, shutting my mouth firmly. I'd had enough of this.

Apparently the judge had, too. Without hesitation, he turned back to Tara and Harvey and announced, "The court finds in favor of the defendant. Case dismissed."

That's torn it, I thought, feeling relief and apprehension in equal measure. Tara would be absolutely one hundred percent furious at me.

The group of ropers was trooping docilely out of the court room. I joined them, keeping my eyes firmly away from Tara. Things might have gone all right if it weren't for Harvey. Clearly seething, both with anger and triumph, he grabbed Tara by the shoulder, just as the group of us emerged into the hallway.

"So how does it feel to know you rode a good horse to death?"

Tara's hands clenched into fists; she looked up at Harvey in direct, murderous fury. However, Harvey was big and looked angry enough to deck her then and there. She contented herself with a "Shut the fuck up, asshole," whirling away as she spoke.

The movement brought her up against me, face to face. I took a step backward, and Tara, seeing a smaller, more vulnerable target, seemed to coil. "You lying bitch."

I took two more fast steps backward, my heart pounding. I'm five foot seven and a reasonably strong human being; I definitely outweighed Tara Hollister. But I've never in my life engaged in a fistfight and I didn't intend to start now.

"I did not lie," I bleated out, sounding for all the world like a startled sheep.

This seemed to inflame Tara; she moved toward me, those red

97

fingernails curling, her mouth stretched tight over her teeth.

I turned and walked. My heart was pounding loud enough to deafen me, my hands shook. I waited for the impact of her leap on my back, but it didn't happen. Only her harsh angry voice taunting after me, "Chickenshit bitch."

I kept walking. My head was literally throbbing with rage. I wanted to tear Tara Hollister limb from limb. I wanted to see her mangled body lying on the floor in front of me.

The thought brought me to myself in a sudden rush. Was this how people murdered? Could I actually kill someone?

Well, no, the other half of my mind said coolly, you couldn't even bring yourself to fight. Of course, it added, that was the right thing to do. It would have been entirely unprofessional for a veterinarian to be seen duking it out with a client in a public place.

But I hate her guts, I answered back. I want to see her locked up and the key thrown away. Sentenced to the electric chair, preferably.

I'd reached the bank of elevators at the end of the hall by this time. I looked back. The group of ropers had disappeared out the front door. Out there was where my truck was, too. But I was damn sure not going in that direction until they were all gone.

I looked back at the elevators. On the third floor of this building was the Santa Cruz County Sheriff's Department offices. Among the people who worked there was a detective, Jeri Ward, whom I could almost consider a friend. That was stretching it a bit. An acquaintance. At any rate, someone who might talk to me.

I pushed the button with the number 3.

THIRTEEN

I felt a little nervous waiting for Detective Ward. After all, I had no business being here. Just a busybody's sort of business. And I wasn't sure, really, if Jeri Ward liked me or thought I was a meddling idiot. It was hard to tell. Our last encounter had been mildly positive. Still, I'd given my name at the desk diffidently, uncertain as to whether Detective Ward would make time for me.

And now I was waiting in a sterile cubicle, wondering what the hell I was doing here. Well, that wasn't quite true. If I was honest with myself, I knew exactly what I was doing here. Making sure Tara wasn't overlooked as a suspect in Jack's murder.

Damn. It struck me that this was a pretty shitty thing to be doing. And that I was doing it primarily because Tara had just embarrassed me in a very public way. All right, I'd done the only reasonable thing, but I still felt like a coward, as Tara had put it to me so much less gracefully. I was getting back at her.

You don't need to do that, I remonstrated, resolving firmly that I would not bring up Tara's name. So then, what was I doing here? Why, clearing Joanna of course, my mind retorted, ever glib. Never mind that I'd pretty much forgotten about

Joanna and hadn't a clue as to how I might clear her, even assuming she needed clearing.

At this enlivening thought the door opened and Detective Jeri Ward stepped into the room. As always, my first impression of her was not positive. A blond woman with short, neatly cut hair, Detective Ward had fair skin and even, unremarkable features. She wore a suit—a quiet navy blue plaid with a white blouse and a red silk tie—and her face matched the clothes. A cool, distanced, professional face with those unnervingly impersonal eyes that most cops seem to have, looking out at me. A power face. This was part of her job, of course, to be in charge, but I still didn't like her demeanor.

As a law-abiding, tax-paying citizen, I tend to find that typical cop-behavior mannerism—you're guilty until proven innocent—annoying, and this woman and I had not gotten along well at all during our first few meetings. As I'd grown to know her a little better, however, I'd realized that her expressionless, aloof manner concealed a fair-minded, intelligent human being, and I'd come to understand that she needed to put her emotions on hold, so to speak, in order to do a good job. Still, I found that superior attitude ("can't trust a member of the goddamned public to do anything right") got under my skin.

"So, Dr. McCarthy, what can I do for you?" Jeri Ward's greeting was formal; no one watching us would have guessed we'd cooperated on two previous problems.

"Hello, Detective Ward, how are you?" I smiled at her and her expression unbent a trifle, the muscles of her face relaxing in almost imperceptible ways.

"I'm fine, Dr. McCarthy, and you?"

"Gail," I said. "I'm okay."

She didn't ask me to call her Jeri—she never had—but she smiled slightly. The smile vanished instantly when I asked, "You've heard about Jack Hollister's murder up in Tahoe?"

Once again Jeri Ward's eyes were the dead, inhuman eyes of a cop. "Yes. I understand you were involved?"

"Sort of. A friend of mine went out to dinner with him the

night he was murdered. The cops were interested in questioning her, naturally. As it happened, I was the one who introduced them, so I got questioned, too. We were all—Jack, Joanna, and I—up there at a veterinary convention."

Jeri Ward nodded intently, making no comment, her silence meant to encourage my talk. I looked back at her, matching her silence with my own, waiting for a question.

"Do you have something to add to the investigation?" she asked me after a moment, her face betraying no sign of our minor skirmish.

"I'm not sure. You probably have all the information I do. I'm mostly concerned about Joanna. She seemed to be the number one suspect for a while, and I feel responsible for that, since I introduced her to Jack." What the hell. It was almost true. Ought to be true.

Jeri Ward regarded me levelly, seeming to look right through the white lie to my less than noble motivations. After a minute, she answered my unspoken question. "Joanna Lund is not a primary suspect at the moment."

"So the gun wouldn't have fit in the purse," I said without thinking.

A flash of surprise unsettled the detective's composure and was gone instantly. "What do you mean, Dr. McCarthy?"

"I wondered, when Joanna described her purse to me, if the gun would have fit inside. That detective up in Tahoe said it was a twenty-two, which could be pretty small, but I figure it would have to have had a silencer on it for the shot to have gone unnoticed."

"Yes." Deliberately, it seemed to me, she added, "The gun was an old long-barreled twenty-two revolver; it was actually about sixteen inches in length—too long to have fit in the purse. The silencer was homemade, a length of lead pipe fitted over the barrel. The shot would have made a sound no louder than snapping your fingers."

"Where did you find it?" I was pushing my luck.

"In the lake." As I had guessed.

"So someone shot Jack in the back of the head without anyone in the casino hearing, pushed his body off the deck and threw the gun into the lake, then walked back into the casino through that back door by the restrooms without a single person noticing a thing. It could have happened in the space of five minutes."

"It's possible."

"And Joanna's purse being out there was strictly a coincidence. Jack probably brought it with him."

"We think that's likely. His fingerprints were on it."

"So whoever did have the gun must have been carrying it in a bigger bag, a suitcase maybe?"

She shrugged. "Or a duffel bag, or a backpack, or a larger purse. An overcoat with a roomy pocket."

"I see. Lots of choices. And whatever it was, it wasn't noticed."

"Apparently not." Jeri Ward looked right into my eyes, her expression hard. "So does this bring any ideas to mind, Dr. McCarthy?"

I thought about it. "Not exactly. Since Jack wasn't robbed, it does make me think he was shot by someone who knew him, who knew or guessed he would be at that casino, and who had a reason to kill him. Do you know the terms of his will?" I was getting around to Tara now.

"Yes."

"His three ex-wives inherit everything equally?"

Again, she looked briefly surprised. "More or less."

"Except the Hollister Ranch, which goes to the state."

"Possibly." Her expression was guarded.

"So the ex-wives have the best motive. Do they have alibis?" Now I was headed for Tara in earnest.

"I'm sorry. That's not information I can give you."

I wasn't surprised. I was a little surprised, though, when she added, "Do you know anyone else who might have a motive to kill Jack Hollister?"

I'd answered this question before, what seemed years ago, in

Tahoe. But I knew considerably more now than I did then. On the other hand, none of it added up to anything but what I'd just said. The three ex-wives had a motive, and of the three, I'd pick Tara every time. But I could hardly say that. Not to mention I'd never met the other two.

Jeri Ward watched me think. When I shook my head negatively, she said, "I happen to be assigned to assist the Washoe County Sheriff's Department on this case. Detective Holmquist and I are conferencing this afternoon."

"He's here?" I was shocked; I'm not sure why. I associated Detective Holmquist strictly with those two miserable days in Tahoe, and the thought of him walking down a sunny Santa Cruz street, perhaps at this very moment, was disconcerting. My mental image—rabbit face, keen mind—raised immediate feelings of nervousness and guilt.

Jeri Ward half smiled. "He'll be here at two o'clock. If there's anything you could add that might help us, I wish you'd tell me now."

I struggled with my emotions a bit—some vestige of a British boys'-school ethic lingering in me, a resistance to "tattling." Logic finally compelled me to say, "Tara Hollister seems to need money pretty badly."

There, now it was out, what I'd really come to do, what I'd promised myself I'd avoid. I'd done it. I'd pointed a finger straight at Tara. Part of me felt like a cowardly, back-stabbing piece of shit. Another part felt vindictively triumphant. I tried to persuade myself that the dominant emotion really was a virtuous, rational desire to assist the cops in any way I could to find Jack's murderer. I didn't believe it, though.

Predictably, Jeri Ward was not about to let this piece of information lie. Instantly she was prodding at it, and at me. "Do you know Tara Hollister?"

"Barely. We're acquaintances." Honesty compelled me to add, "We don't like each other much." I probably should have told Detective Ward that Tara had virtually attacked me in this very building not an hour ago, that was how much we didn't like each

103

other, but I couldn't bring myself to do it. I felt enough of a fool already.

"Scuttlebutt has it that Tara's gone through the money she got from the divorce, and it certainly seems to be the case. That's all I really know." The sheriff's department was not going to be interested in my inward conviction that Tara was an amoral person—one who could kill. She'd ridden a horse to death and had no more sense of the wrongness of what she'd done than a cat who tortures a quail. She had both a motive and the temperament for murdering Jack—what more did they want?

Opportunity, and evidence linking her to the scene of the crime, no doubt, but there was no way Jeri Ward was going to discuss those issues with me, the meddling amateur sleuth. I decided to risk one more question.

"Who was the gun registered to?"

Jeri thought about that awhile and finally decided to answer. "The serial numbers were filed off." Her curt tone indicated that was the last piece of information I was getting, and she stood up as she spoke. Our interview was at an end.

I stood up, too, and thanked her for her time, promised to let her know if any relevant information came my way. On my way out of the county building, I checked carefully for signs of Tara, but I'd killed a full hour in the sheriff-coroner's office, and the ropers were all long gone.

Good thing. I started my truck, glancing regretfully at the sunny blue day outside the windows. Time to get my mind back on work. In ten minutes, I'd be back at the veterinary clinic. My real job, so long neglected, loomed ahead.

FOURTEEN

It was almost two o'clock when I pulled in the driveway of Santa Cruz Equine Practice. Hardly an early start to a working day. Of course, Jim had known I needed to attend the trial; that didn't mean he liked it.

I scanned the parking lot somewhat anxiously. Jim's truck was missing; I relaxed. I definitely preferred to skip my boss's usual caustic comments over what had taken me so long.

Getting out of the truck, I looked around at my place of employment, which seemed oddly unfamiliar after a week's absence. I could almost see the small complex through a stranger's eyes: the blocky, ungraceful clinic with its garagelike metal roll-up doors in the rear, the row of stalls and pens, the level dirt area we used for unloading and jogging horses. As I trudged toward the back door, I was struck by the fact that the whole place had an institutional quality that was profoundly unhorsy.

If I ever had my own clinic, a big if, I'd devote at least a little time and money to making it look friendly. A strip of cottage flowers by the front door, maybe; a patch of green grass where visiting horses could relax and snatch a snack. I'd paint my shed row barn red instead of government-standard beige and try, in every small way I could, to make the place seem like someone's barnyard that just happened to be an animal hospital.

In my early days here, I'd suggested this approach to Jim, but I hadn't gotten anywhere. Spending money on unnecessary frills wasn't Jim's way. In fact, spending money on anything wasn't Jim's way. I had to lobby hard to get outdated, unreliable equipment replaced; it had taken me a year to talk him into putting a car phone in my truck, a convenience that had saved me an enormous amount of time. Jim liked to make money, not spend it.

I walked in the back door to be greeted with cordial reserve by the tech and the two receptionists, none of whom I knew well. Jim insisted on a severe distinction between us two, as the veterinarians, and the rest of the staff; he had warned me when I went to work for him that he didn't want me hanging out with "the help."

I had mixed emotions about this. In some ways it struck me as a ridiculous, old-fashioned attitude, a good deal too snobbish for my taste, but nearly three years of working at the clinic had demonstrated his reasoning fairly effectively. Office politics created an enormous amount of trouble; receptionists and technicians sniped at each other and feuded over minor points of power, alliances were formed and broken with unceasing regularity, and the staff's natural inclination to make off-duty friendships resulted in hostilities over stolen boyfriends and the like.

By nature I was reserved; between my own inability to banter easily and Jim's strictures, I'd found it simpler to stay slightly aloof, a technique that had, in the end, proved more useful than otherwise. Sometimes, though, like now, I wished things were different, that the three women of various ages greeting me with variations on "Hi, Gail; how was the seminar?" were friends instead of acquaintances. It would have been nice to flop down at my desk and tell somebody all about Jack's murder, my own involvement, and that ridiculous scene with Tara. It might have put everything into proportion, and I certainly would have felt more connected, less isolated.

Instead I told them that the seminar had been all right and asked how things were going at the clinic. "Slow" was the answer. Jim was a bear, the tech said. I wasn't surprised. Jim hated it when things were slow—not enough money coming in. On the other hand, at least he shouldn't be too annoyed about work stacking up during my absence.

I started to sit down at my desk and look for the schedule Jim had undoubtedly left, when the phone rang. The younger receptionist hurried to answer it. She was gone only a minute and then dashed back into the small cubicle I used as an office with agitation written large on her face.

"Gail, Kris Griffith needs you right away. Something bad's wrong with Rebby; he's all uncoordinated. She said he just fell down."

Oh shit. I'd completely forgotten about Kris and Rebby, and Rebby's odd way of moving near the end of the endurance race. I'd meant to call and check on him and never done it. Damn.

"Call and tell Kris I'm on my way," I told the girl. She was eighteen and part-time, one of many kids who worked at the clinic because they intended to become veterinarians someday. This one was also involved in endurance riding and knew Kris a little. I could tell by the degree of upset she was showing that Kris was probably really stressed out about Reb.

Jumping back into the truck, I headed down Soquel Drive, all thoughts of lunch and checking the schedule vanishing into an overwhelming worry. What in the hell was wrong with Rebby?

Never theorize in advance of the facts, I reminded myself, but I kept replaying in my mind his odd way of trotting on Saturday. The hind legs had swung awkwardly out, as if he'd lost some control of them.

When I pulled into Kris's barnyard ten minutes later, I had to remind myself to be calm and unemotional—only in that frame of mind could I do a good job.

Kris had herself on a tight rein; tension showed in every line of her face and body, but she kept to a terse recital of the facts as we walked to the pen behind the barn.

"He seems to be getting worse, Gail. When I brought him home from the ride I kept a close eye on him, and he was swinging his hind legs out in an odd way, but that was it. Yesterday it seemed even more pronounced, but he didn't seem to be in any pain and he was eating well and looked bright, so I thought I'd just watch him. And then, this afternoon, when I went out to check him, he was loping across the corral, bucking a little and playing, like he does and he just fell down. It was like he lost control of his back legs or something. I couldn't believe it. That horse has never fallen. Never."

By this time we'd reached the corral and I was watching Rebby, who was walking to greet us. As the horse approached, I felt consternation and dismay growing in the pit of my stomach. Always a graceful mover, he seemed, overnight, to have become incredibly awkward, swinging his back legs in a loose disjointed way and stumbling every dozen or so steps.

Kris caught him and led him back and forth a few times so I could study him, and the condition seemed if anything to grow more pronounced. "Did he get this bad very suddenly?" I asked.

Kris looked as worried and miserable as I was feeling. "I don't know, Gail. Just this morning, I think. He didn't look like this yesterday. But it's such an odd thing; I've never seen anything like it before, and I'm just not sure."

I stared at Rebby, feeling worse and worse. What came to my mind was "wobbler syndrome," and I didn't want to say the words.

Wobbler syndrome, a complex neurological problem that causes horses to stagger in more or less this way, is caused by malformed vertebrae in the neck. It's thought, at least at the present time, to be a condition that exists at birth, and is merely "activated" by the stress of training. Commonly its onset occurs when a young horse begins his working life. However, it can occur at any age, and though there is an operation that sometimes reduces the degree of incoordination, this operation is not always successful, and wobbler syndrome is frequently the death knell for the horse in question. And the horse in question was Rebby. Rebby wasn't just a horse; he was a friend. I'd boarded Gunner at Kris's place for a year, and I'd gotten to know Reb as well as I had Kris. The big dark brown gelding was as friendly as a puppy, often stretching his head out toward me in a bid for affection, as he was doing now. Automatically, I stepped up to him and rubbed his forehead, and after a minute he leaned his head on my shoulder and stood there contentedly.

Rubbing the underside of his neck, I said, "I think what's wrong with this horse may be neurological."

"He's only ten," Kris said bleakly. "And he's always been sound."

"I need to do some tests on him."

I reached for the lead rope, but Kris held it tight, fixing her eyes on my face. "What do you think is wrong with him?"

I wondered if I should mention wobbler syndrome and decided not to. No point in scaring Kris until I did the tests. "I'm not sure yet," I said.

Kris still clung to the horse's lead rope. "I'm just afraid you're going to tell me he's got some terrible neurological problem that's incurable and will just get progressively worse and the only thing to do is put him down."

I was silent. Wobbler syndrome is, more or less, a terrible neurological problem that tends to get progressively worse. Kris's fears could be right on the mark.

After a moment I said gently, "We need a diagnosis. We can't proceed in any direction until we have an idea what's wrong with him."

"You're right, I know." Kris blinked rapidly several times and handed me the end of the rope. "Go ahead."

For the next hour, I ran through every neurological test I'd ever done, or heard of. I poked and prodded every inch of

Rebby's neck and spine with the blunt end of my ballpoint pen. I walked and trotted him in small circles, I pulled him off balance by jerking his tail sideways, I walked him up and down slopes, I backed him up, and I blindfolded him and repeated the backup. As I proceeded, I grew more and more certain that my initial diagnosis was wrong. Rebby didn't have the classic loss of balance characteristic of wobbler syndrome; none of my tests gave him much trouble.

"Well, he's not a wobbler," I said when I was done.

Kris nodded in relief. I knew she was horsewoman enough to have suspected the same thing I did.

"Let me try a few other things. Maybe what's wrong with him is injury-related."

"Anything you say, Gail."

I spent another hour examining Reb as carefully as I could for various lamenesses. I flexed and compressed and stretched his stifles and his hocks, I ran my fingers over every one of his vertebrae, I encased my arm in a plastic sheath and reached up his rectum to examine his pelvis. Nothing. He didn't seem to be in pain, in any obvious sense. But his odd way of swinging his hind legs out and strange incoordination remained as pronounced as ever. I felt stumped. Searching back through the file folders of my mind, I tried to remember one of the lectures I'd heard at Tahoe.

Rebby stood quietly on the end of the lead rope, watching me, his eye calm, his demeanor relaxed. He'd been poked and prodded and stretched and palpated in various ways for several hours now, but his equanimity remained unimpaired. I stroked his shoulder. His dark brown coat looked glossy black in the late afternoon light—like many mostly Thoroughbred horses he didn't tend to grow much winter coat.

"EPM," I said out loud.

Kris, understandably, was looking pretty confused at this point. "What's EPM?" she asked.

"Equine protozoal myelopathy," I said. "It's pretty new. Or

110

actually, we're just discovering that it exists and just beginning to find out how to diagnose it and treat it. I learned a little more about it up in Tahoe. "What it is, is a protozoan that gets in the horse's bloodstream; no one knows exactly how. But it can get in the spinal cord and cause symptoms of incoordination like what Rebby is showing."

Getting a needle and syringe from the truck, I drew some blood from Rebby's jugular vein. He stood quietly for this procedure, as he had for all the others, his basic trust in human beings overcoming his distaste for the needle.

"I'm going to run a blood test on him," I told Kris. "That will tell us if he's positive for EPM. Meanwhile . . ." I handed her two bottles of pills. "One's an antibiotic and one's a human malaria drug. The dosages are written on the labels. Dissolve them with water and mix them with a little sweet feed. Make sure he eats them."

Kris nodded, familiar with the process of giving pills to horses. Straightening Rebby's forelock where it lay between his eyes, she said hesitantly, "And if he's positive for EPM, these will cure him?"

My turn to hesitate. "Maybe. The thing about EPM is it's unpredictable, not to mention no one seems to understand how it works exactly. It can sometimes get in the spinal cord and cause permanent nerve damage. That's why it's important to get him on the medication right away, just in case he does have EPM. Put him in a small pen, too, where he can't run around and fall down and hurt himself. We'll reevaluate as soon as I get the results of the blood test."

"Okay." Kris led Rebby off toward the barn. The aberrant wobble in his long stride was distressing to see, and I felt my throat tighten as I watched him.

When I left, half an hour later, after repeating everything I'd heard about EPM twice more and promising to call in the morning and check on Reb, it was almost five o'clock. Dutifully I

111

rang the office; five might be official quitting time, but for a veterinarian, the day's over when the calls are done, not before.

I knew by the sound of the receptionist's voice that it was bad, even before I really understood what she was saying. "Gail, there's an emergency in Watsonville. Some horse got hit by a car on Apple Lane. The girl called; she says the horse is all bloody, but it's still moving. She thinks it's alive."

FIFTEEN

I drove toward Apple Lane praying. Please God, don't let this be too bad. Don't let me find this horse in terrible pain. I'd been a vet for almost three years now, but I'd never grown used to dealing with terminally suffering horses. The best thing I could do was put them out of their misery, but it was never easy.

I knew Apple Lane, a short side street in the orchards behind Watsonville, and the accident scene was obvious. The blinking yellow flashers on the car by the side of the road, sharp in the twilight, drew me like a magnet. I took a deep breath as I got out of the truck. Hold it together, Gail; just hold it together.

I walked toward the little knot of people standing by the car. I registered an older woman, a middle-aged man, and a teenage girl. Then I saw the horse.

It was on the verge, screened from passing traffic by the car and people. I knew instantly that it was dead. There is a certain stillness, a flatness to a dead animal. I let out my breath in relief.

Dead was bad, but suffering was worse. I approached the group of people. No hurry now.

The girl didn't know that, though. She'd spotted me and ran in my direction, grabbing my arm and pulling me toward the horse's body. "Please, you're the vet, aren't you? Come look at her. She's not dead. She was moving."

I followed the girl.

There was a lot of blood. Dark and viscous, it was puddled on the pavement, looking black in the colorless light of dusk. I could see where the car had plowed into the front end of the mare's body, causing the gaping wounds in her shoulder and what looked like a broken right front leg. But it was the head injury, I thought, as I stooped down, that had killed her. The back of her skull was crushed.

Even though I was sure, I pressed my fingers to the horse's jugular vein for a full minute, wanting to comfort the girl. "She's dead," I said, as gently as I could.

"She can't be. She was moving."

"They do that," I explained. "Even after the brain is dead, the body makes little involuntary movements. They're automatic, reflexive." I searched for the right words. "She wasn't in pain, or anything. She died of this head injury. It was probably pretty sudden and painless for her."

The girl gulped and nodded, holding herself together with an effort. She was about fifteen and had a sweet, immature face, the sort of teenager who was still more interested in horses than boys. And this was her worst nightmare come true.

"I was just letting her eat grass here along the driveway. She loves the green grass. Something scared her and she jerked the lead rope out of my hand and ran out on the road. Her name's Mandy." Sobs were overtaking the words.

I looked around frantically at the two adults behind us, and the man stepped forward and put his arm around the girl. "It's okay, Shelly. There's nothing we can do."

"Are you her father?"

"Yes."

"I think it would be better if you got her away from here. It can't be helping her to look at her horse like this."

He nodded and shepherded the girl off. I turned to the woman. She said quietly, "I hit the horse. It wasn't my fault; the

damn thing ran right in front of my car. I didn't see it coming."
I looked where she pointed; a large, dense holly bush obscured the driveway entrance completely.
"It just ran out from behind that bush as I came by. I didn't have a chance to miss it."
I nodded. I didn't blame her.
"My car's a wreck."
Sure enough—the front end of the station wagon was completely crumpled.
"It's really these people's fault," she went on, "but I feel terrible."
"Are you all right?" I asked her.
"Oh, physically, yes. I was wearing my seatbelt. I'm fine. I just feel sick about the poor horse, and that little girl."
"I know," I said inadequately.
"I guess I'd better get their name and number and insurance and all that." She sounded tired and sad.
"Yes. And probably call the cops."
"And a tow truck."
"I've got a car phone in my pickup," I told her. "You're welcome to use it."
"Thank you."
The next half hour passed in the dull trivia that follows tragedy. Numerous phone calls and consultations took place. I got a tarp out of my truck and covered the mare's body.
Cops arrived; so did a fire truck and an ambulance, which were sent on their way. The girl's father returned, helpful and apologetic. Nobody wanted to sue anybody. A little of my faith in human nature was restored.
Details got taken care of one by one, but eventually I realized no one had a clue what to do about the mare's body.
"Shall I call the tallow truck for you?" I asked.
The man, who had turned out to be one Bob Walford, gulped a little over this. "Poor Shelly," he said anxiously. "She'd hate that."
"You've got to do something with the body," I pointed out.

"You could bury her, if you've got a place that's suitable and a backhoe handy, though I believe it's technically illegal."

"No, no we can't do that. I guess you'd better call the . . . what do you call it?"

"The tallow truck."

"What does it cost?"

"It's free. He makes his money on the carcass."

It sounded brutal, I knew. But what else was there to say? The mare was gone; the living creature the girl had called Mandy had fled. All that remained was inanimate, dead flesh, the waste of her empty body, which did need to be disposed of.

I arranged for the truck to come, and eventually got myself disentangled. I'd felt I'd been there for hours and was amazed that the dashboard clock only said six.

Jesus, what a day. I needed a break.

Stopping at a little Mexican restaurant down the road, I ordered a margarita from the waitress. "On the rocks, Cuervo Gold, fresh lime juice and lots of salt."

I had two of them, then ordered an enchilada, though I wasn't really hungry. Sometimes it seemed that all there was to being a veterinarian was facing tragedy head-on. There would be better days, I knew, days when I saved lives and saw tears of joy on my clients' faces, rather than tears of sorrow, but they seemed far away. I stared at the painting of a bullfighter on black velvet that hung on the wall next to my table and wondered, not for the first time, if I'd chosen the right profession.

I got home an hour later feeling drained and sad. The welcome jingle of Blue's collar on the other side of the door as I unlocked it announced that he was fine, and Bonner came scooting in from parts unknown with a loud meow, slithering between me and the dog as I walked in the house.

Relief, deep as it was temporary, filled my heart. I rubbed Blue's head, then took him outside for his required walk. For the moment, at least, my little animal family was okay. Gunner and Plumber were safe with Lonny; the cat and dog were here with me. The dark, twisted thing that coils in our very cells,

116

human as well as animal, that waits on the highways and lurks in the weather, the thing that had reached out and laid a finger on Rebby and taken the girl's Mandy, was elsewhere tonight. Soon I would grapple with it again; for all I knew my first call tomorrow would be another life-and-death struggle, but for now I tumbled into bed and fell instantly asleep, my mind empty of everything but sheer fatigue.

SIXTEEN

At six the next morning, I got up, climbed my ladder stairway to the kitchen and made a pot of coffee, then showered and dressed. By the time I'd settled myself at the end of the couch with my favorite blue willow cup steaming into the cold air of the living room, first light was just graying the ridge top. Picking up the phone, I dialed Kris's number, hoping Rick wouldn't answer.

"Hello?" It was Kris.

"It's Gail. So how are you doing?"

"Okay."

"How's Reb?"

"The same." Her voice was flat.

"What did Rick say when you told him?" Kris's husband, though wealthy, had a marked aversion to spending money on medical treatment for horses.

"I didn't tell him. Rick couldn't care less whether Reb lives or dies. He's already gone to work." Kris's tone was bitter.

I was startled. I didn't like Rick Griffith at all. I thought his good looks and superficial charm thinly masked a domineering and aggressive personality, and I noticed that Kris seemed dimmed in his presence, her normally forthright manner growing several shades more submissive. But I'd never heard her acknowledge any resentment toward him before. I'd always assumed she was unaware or unconcerned with the (to me) unpleasant dynamics between them, and simply enjoyed Rick's obvious looks, wealth, and, let's say, forcefully polite manners, well enough. Apparently I was wrong.

"Is something going on with you and Rick?" I asked hesitantly.

"Oh, just the usual; nothing in common anymore. Not to mention I'm sure he has a girlfriend."

"Do you care?"

"I don't know. The one thing I do know is he'd fight me like a son-of-a-bitch for custody, and I'd never be able to keep the place, either. I'm not sure a divorce would be worth it."

"Oh." I was silent, thanking my lucky stars I was single and dependent on no one but myself for what I had. Losing her daughter, her property, her security—it would be a big price for Kris to pay. "I'm sorry," I said at last. "I didn't know things were like that."

Kris caught my awkwardness and jumped in. "There's nothing anyone can do. It's not that bad. Anyway, you'll call me when the blood work comes back."

"Right away," I said.

"Thanks, Gail." Kris hung up quickly.

I hesitated a second, then looked Joanna's number up in my personal book and resolutely dialed it. Joanna was a vet and no doubt operated on a schedule just like mine; early in the morning was probably the best time to call her. She answered on the second ring, sounding reasonably alert and cheerful. "Hello?"

"Hi, Joanna, it's Gail." Despite my good intentions, I was sure the primary emotion in my voice was the discomfort I was feeling. Striving for a more upbeat tone, I asked, "So, how are you doing?"

"Good." Joanna's tone was as emphatic as my own. "I'm doing good."

"Well, I was worried about you, after all you went through

119

up there in Tahoe," I fumbled, hoping I was saying approximately the right thing.

Silence on the other end of the phone. Joanna's voice, when it finally came, sounded cool. "I'm doing better now."

Resisting the impulse to say, I hope you're getting over what's his name, I asked, "Keeping busy?"

"With this job, you don't have a lot of choice."

I certainly knew about that. "Uh, Joanna," I blurted out, "what did Jack talk about that night you went out to dinner?"

More silence. Then, "You're not still worrying about that, are you?"

"Sort of." I didn't feel like mentioning that I hadn't done a whole lot of good so far; my chief contribution had been an attempt to implicate Tara, a woman I had no real reason to suspect other than pure dislike. "Did Jack say anything that night, anything about his life and what he was doing—anything about anything?" I added lamely.

"He talked a lot about himself," Joanna said, "but I didn't really listen."

"Did he say anything about any of his ex-wives?" I asked, grasping at straws.

"No." Very brusque. "He just talked a lot about some big land deal he was working on that would make him all this money. I mean, I'm sorry he's dead and all that, but he sure went on and on about himself and his deals. He bored me, pretty much. That's all I know." Joanna's tone had grown decidedly curt.

"If you think of anything else," I asked her, "call me, okay?"

"Okay." I barely heard her hasty good-bye as she hung up the phone.

The clock on the wall said quarter after seven. I got up and ran a comb through the damp tangle of my hair, then pulled my boots on. Calling for Blue, I headed out the door.

When I reached the office; Jim's pickup was in the parking lot, though it was only seven-thirty, and we were all due in at eight. No one else was there.

Going in the back door, I greeted my boss, who was sitting

at his desk, compiling the day's schedule. I sat down next to him. "Gail. Good to see you back at work." There was the faintest sarcastic edge to his voice. In theory, Jim had agreed that it was a good idea for me to attend the Winter Equine Seminar and work the endurance ride, and he'd been willing for me to take Monday morning off to attend the trial. But in practice I knew he'd rather I spent twenty-four hours a day down at the clinic, working my butt off. To be fair, this was the schedule he more or less followed himself; Jim was a working fool.

In the three years he'd employed me, I'd had no vacation time other than the seminar, and I worked an average of six days a week, ten hours a day. Nothing in my veterinary training had prepared me for this sort of schedule, nor for the fact that Jim was as tight with money as he was generous with hours. Still, whenever I grew frustrated it always came down to the same bottom line: I couldn't afford to set up a practice of my own, I was committed to living in Santa Cruz County, and Jim was the only decent horse vet in the area. On the plus side, he was more than a decent diagnostician, he was a great one. I'd learned more from him in three years than I had the whole time I was at vet school, and I continued to learn all the time. That in itself was worth a lot of grief.

We discussed Rebby's odd condition for a while. Jim agreed that EPM seemed as likely a diagnosis as any, given the circumstances, but like me, had had little experience diagnosing and treating it. "Let me know how it goes," he said.

Turning back to the schedule, which he had been finishing as we spoke, he ran one square, stubby finger down the page, pointing out several calls he'd set up for me, explaining the ongoing problems he was dealing with. He never looked at me as he talked; his eyes stayed on the page, his square, stocky body shouldered me out of his space unconsciously. I had to virtually peer around him to see what he was pointing at.

One thing about Jim: sexual harassment was not a factor. I wasn't sure he was aware I was a woman; he certainly wasn't interested in me in that sense. He had a wife and four kids, but

121

it was more than good, old-fashioned monogamy. Jim didn't really see me as a person, merely a tool.

I'd gotten used to this, in a way I even liked it. I did my job as well as I could, which he expected and demanded, and that was that. We weren't friends. I accepted that he wouldn't pay a penny more than he had to. End of story.

It didn't surprise me, though, that he'd gone through a junior vet a year before I came along, and that the office and barn staff came and went with unceasing regularity. Jim was not an easy man to work for, by most folks' standards.

"You heard about what happened up at the seminar?" I asked him.

"Jack Hollister got killed. Yeah, I heard."

Jim was never talkative, but this was oddly brusque, even for him. "Did you know Jack?" I ventured.

"Yeah, I knew him." Jim stared at the list on his desk, eyes cast firmly down, mouth a straight, expressionless line.

"I take it you weren't friends."

Jim shrugged. "He tried to put me out of business when I moved here—it must be twenty years ago now."

I was shocked. "Why?"

"He didn't want me poaching on his territory. He told everybody he knew, which was everybody in the county who owned a horse, pretty much, that I was no good as a veterinarian."

This didn't sound like Jack to me. And yet, I reminded myself, how well had I really known the man?

"Eventually people figured out I wasn't so bad and I got a few clients, and Jack got so rich buying and selling ranches he retired. But no, we weren't friends. Of course, I'm sorry he was murdered." Jim didn't sound terribly sorry. "Now about this mare you need to preg check up in Felton . . ." He launched into the reproductive history of the horse in question, but I wasn't really listening.

Easygoing, handsome, wealthy, flirtatious Jack Hollister—everybody's friend—that was how I had seen Jack. The sort of vindictive, petty behavior Jim was describing didn't fit my picture at all. And yet, Jim had no reason to lie.

"There's a gelding in Aptos who needs his teeth floated . . ." Jim was still talking. I tried to focus on what he was saying when we both heard the noisy rattle of a truck and trailer pulling into the back parking lot.

"Damn." Jim said it with feeling and I knew what he was thinking. An unscheduled emergency—the client had simply hauled the horse down without calling, assuming we'd be here. Not a good start to the day.

Before either of us could get up and start out the door, a figure burst through it, talking volubly in my direction as he came. "I need you to come with me right now. That goddamn Tara stole Willy and I need a witness."

It was Bronc, as agitated as I'd ever seen him.

"Come on," he said, grabbing my elbow and propelling me toward the door.

"What are you talking about, Bronc," I said firmly, digging my heels in. "And why do you need me?"

"Because I need a witness, goddammit, when I take the son-of-a-bitch away from her. Someone who knows Willy and knows he's my horse. The closest goddamned brand inspector is in Salinas and I don't have time for that. Now, come on."

I looked at Jim and was amused, even under the circumstances, to see that his usual rocklike composure had deserted him; his face looked startled and aghast. "You'd better go," he said.

I made one last-ditch effort. "Bronc, what you need is the police."

"I do not need any goddamn cops. Now are you going or not, 'cause if you're not I'm going without you and if I kill that bitch it's on your head."

"I'm going, I'm going." Following him out the door, I gave a moment's thought to the wisdom of this course, but dismissed it with a mental shrug. Oh well. Looked like I was on board.

Five minutes later I wished I'd thought harder. Bronc was driving eighty miles an hour plus down the freeway, the stock trailer rattling wildly behind us. I wedged myself into the corner of the seat, searching for a seatbelt; either the old one-ton pickup didn't have them or they were buried out of reach.

"Slow down, Bronc," I commanded.

No result except he stepped on the accelerator. "That bitch is not gonna steal that horse and get away with it," he muttered.

Closing my eyes as the speedometer crept up toward ninety, I said, "Bronc, if you don't slow down, I am jumping out of this truck at the first stop sign and finding my own way back to the clinic."

I could hear him smile, that quick wolfish smile, as he said, "I ain't gonna kill you, honey."

"I don't care. Slow down or I'm getting out as soon as I can."

"This okay?"

I opened my eyes to find the speedometer at seventy; we were already halfway to Watsonville and, thankfully, the freeway was reasonably empty.

"Okay, but no faster," I said firmly.

"Deal."

Shit. Some deal. I stared out the window at the Monterey Bay, vividly blue in the winter sunshine, the towers of the power plant standing out sharp and tall at Moss Landing, many miles away. Santa Cruz County was at its best in the winter, I sometimes thought; the scenery outside the window was markedly lovely—too bad it was passing so damn fast.

"Bronc," I warned. The speedometer had risen to eighty while I looked away.

His foot lifted ever so slightly off the gas pedal and I asked him peevishly, "What in the hell is the point of going so fast?"

"I don't want that bitch to have time to move the horse."

"How do you know it was Tara who stole him? How do you know he was even stolen? Maybe he got out."

Bronc looked at me and looked back at the road, appearing

by his expression to be pondering the stupidity of women in general.

"Wire was cut," he said curtly. "Down by the road where I can't see the fence from the house. There were tire tracks outside the fence in the wet ground. A few of Willy's hoofprints. Someone cut the fence and led him out and loaded him in a trailer."

"How do you know it was Tara?"

"I know, all right," was all he would say.

"So, where exactly is it we're going?" I asked him as he took the Elkhorn Slough exit.

"Right smack up to the bitch's front door." Bronc's face had a hard set to it and his voice held a quality I'd never quite heard from him before. Another question occurred to me.

"You don't have a gun, do you?"

For a second he looked startled; it appeared if he was contemplating mayhem it wasn't of that sort.

"Naw, I don't have a gun. If I kill her it'll be with my bare hands." The humorous tone had returned to his voice, but the other quality was still there. I began to worry in earnest.

Bronc was pulling the trailer down a long dirt driveway—a pair of muddy ruts barely encrusted with gravel. Crooked board corrals lined the drive, which led to a house I would be inclined to call a shack. It wasn't that my own abode was any bigger or more intrinsically glamorous, it was just that this place was so palpably uncared for. The paint was faded and peeling, the rough patch of lawn unmowed, pieces of rusting junk everywhere. Behind the house stood a big, old barn, and it was on this building that Bronc's eyes were fixed as he climbed out of the truck. Without a word he began to walk toward it.

Not having any better ideas, I followed him.

Tara's truck, with a trailer hitched to it, was parked in front of the barn. Tara herself came out of the open barn doorway and planted her body in front of Bronc as he strode toward her.

"What the hell are you doing here?"

"I came to get my horse." Bronc faced her without an atom of give; I had the sense he would have just tossed her out of the way and gone on if I hadn't been there.

"What horse?"

"My buckskin gelding."

"I don't have him."

"I'm gonna walk through your barn and see."

"You damn well are not."

Tara stepped inside the doorway of the barn and reappeared almost instantly. To my absolute disbelief she was holding a gun. Moreover, she was pointing it straight at us. In sick fascination my eyes fixed themselves on the round black hole at the end of the barrel. *Oh my God* were the only words that came to mind.

"You all better stop right there," Tara ordered.

Her voice sounded shrill with strain, and my eyes flew up to her face. Tense and jittery, her expression gave me no confidence that she knew better than to shoot us.

Stopping obediently, I raised both hands placatingly in the air. Bronc, however, kept walking.

"You stop, you son-of-a-bitch, or you're dead. This is my property and you're trespassing." Tara pointed the gun right at the center of Bronc's body.

He kept walking toward her as if he hadn't heard; my heart thudded a steady, frightened tattoo.

Tara sighted down the barrel; I could see her finger tighten on the trigger.

"For God's sake!" The words burst out of my mouth.

They startled Tara and her eyes leapt to me. In that split second, Bronc lunged forward and grabbed at her. With a loud crack, the gun went off.

I was already flinging myself to the ground, face down, heart pounding fit to jump out of my chest. Oh shit. Oh my God.

I had no idea where the bullet went, no idea, really, if I'd been hit. For a moment, I just lay there in the dirt, shocked out of my wits.

Scuffling and shouting came from Tara's direction, but no more shots. I lifted my head cautiously.

Bronc held the gun in one hand and Tara with the other. His arm was wrapped around her neck, her throat in the crook of his elbow, her feet almost off the ground. He held the gun away from her, pointing it up into space. I got slowly to my feet.

"Come get this thing," he said, sounding a little out of breath, but completely unflustered.

Walking over to him, I gingerly took the pistol from his hand, noticing that my own hand was shaking.

"Now hold that gun on her while I go check the barn."

Oh great. What was I supposed to do, shoot her if she went after him?

"And you," he gave Tara a shake, causing her to emit a choked shriek, "you stay here."

He let go of her and she slumped to her knees, her hands going immediately to her throat, rubbing it protectively. I had an idea Bronc had squeezed pretty hard.

Staring at the gun in my hand, not really believing the position I was in, I pointed it up in the air as Bronc had done. It was a long-barreled, old-fashioned-looking twenty-two revolver, I saw, similar to the gun that had shot Jack, according to what Jeri Ward told me. Had Tara owned a pair perhaps? Of course, I reminded myself, it was hardly an uncommon gun.

Tara was getting to her feet. She cast a glance at me and I wondered if I should train the gun on her, but rejected the idea instantly. The whole situation was ridiculous—a frightening farce. I was certainly not going to shoot Tara.

Seeing that I had no apparent intention of pointing the gun her way, Tara headed into the barn, looking back over her shoulder at me as she went. I could hear her voice raised at Bronc, sounding angry, but frightened, too.

"That's not him. That's my new boarder. Get your hands off of him."

"Go to hell. I'd know this horse anywhere."

In another minute Bronc emerged, leading a muddy brown gelding with a roached mane and bobbed tail. It took me a minute, but I finally recognized Willy. Tara had obviously been hard at work with hair dye, scissors, and clippers.

She was gesticulating wildly at Bronc as he led the horse away from the barn, but everything—gestures, words, facial expression—lacked force. Tara was beaten and she knew it.

Bronc loaded Willy in the trailer over her objections. Turning to face her, he spoke with a kind of level hardness, that same expression I'd glimpsed in the pickup. "Shut your mouth. This is my horse and you know it and I know it. I don't want to hear any more bullshit about it. You know damn well Jack left the horse to me, otherwise you wouldn't have bothered to steal him. Now I'm telling you something. I'm not going to say a word about this. It's up to you." And with that, he gestured at me to get in the truck.

I wasn't quite ready. I still held the twenty-two in my hand and it gave me a certain sense of power. Not to mention Tara looked shaken; for the first time in our acquaintance her rough-edged, hostile attitude had been replaced by a slightly hangdog expression. Now, I figured, was the right time for some questions.

"Why let her off the hook?" I said to Bronc. And looking straight at Tara as I tipped the barrel of the pistol slightly, I asked her, "So where were you the night Jack was killed?"

Her head jerked up at that. "Not in Tahoe," she said, "and I can prove it. I had a party here. Mike and Dave and Ray and Ray's new girlfriend were all over. They ended up sleeping here. I've got an alibi."

Well, well, well. From the sound of her voice she'd told this story before; I could guess to whom. Though Mike and Dave and Ray were low-lifes who could surely be induced to lie for money, the probability that she'd bribe them all seemed slight. Of course, there was always the possibility that she'd hired a killer and arranged her alibi on purpose.

"I didn't kill Jack, she announced defensively, "and anybody who says I did is a liar."

"You did know the terms of his will, though, and I see you've got a gun."

"So what?" Once again the normally bombastic Tara looked confused.

"You'll inherit a bunch," I said mildly.

"Yeah, but when?" The frustration in Tara's voice was clearly deeply felt. She seemed too upset to deny what was obviously a strong motive. "I need some money soon. I can't even afford to buy a stupid horse." For a moment she sounded very young, and I almost felt sorry for her. Almost but not quite. It wasn't lost on me that her poverty was her own doing, and the fact that she didn't have a horse had a lot to do with the fact that she'd ridden the last one to death.

I looked at her, standing there in her shabby driveway, having just attempted to steal a good horse away from its rightful owner and wondered what in the world would become of her. With her natural belligerence in abeyance she seemed a supremely pathetic creature—a stupid, trashy, criminal waste of a human being, doomed to be nothing but a burden to herself and others. Her only asset—a minimal sort of female beauty—was fading fast; age and hard living would rapidly erase the face and figure that had won Jack's heart. And then what?

Well, she'd be rich. That is, if she wasn't in jail for murder.

Tara seemed to read my thoughts. "I didn't kill the bastard," she said, with a return of her usual defensive hostility. "But I'm sure grateful to whoever did."

"You done?" Bronc asked me, looking disgusted. He'd listened to our exchange silently, leaning on the pickup and waiting, but Tara's last comment seemed to be too much for him. He appeared ready to wring her neck then and there.

"Yeah, I guess so." I set the pistol down gingerly in the rough grass at the edge of the driveway and started to climb into the truck, still looking back at Tara, feeling there must be something more to do or say.

Bronc had no such inhibitions. Jumping in the driver's side, he started the engine and rattled off down the driveway without a second glance. I watched Tara through the rearview mirror the whole time, but she made no attempt to pick up the gun, just stood there staring after us.

"Do you think she killed Jack or had him killed?" I asked Bronc as we pulled back on the county road.

"How the hell would I know? She's a nasty piece of work, that's for sure."

"Bronc, do you have any idea who might have killed Jack?"

"No, honey, I don't. Jack had a finger in a lot of pies and I didn't know about all of them. All I know is it's a damn shame he's dead."

"You and Trav have alibis, anyway." I said it lightly, but I was curious to see what he'd say.

"That's right." Bronc looked at me sharply. "You been talking to the kid?"

"A little."

He was quiet for a second. "Leave Travis alone, sweetheart," he said finally. "He's taking this pretty hard."

His words made me ashamed of myself. What business did I have bothering these people? "What are you going to do about Willy?" I asked him, trying to change the subject.

"Nothing."

"People are going to wonder why you dyed him brown and cut off his mane and tail."

"Let 'em wonder."

Really, I thought, in some ways Bronc was just plain impossible. Soft-hearted about Travis one minute and completely irascible the next. Never mind that mostly I liked and admired the cantankerous old fart; his cowboy code of ethics could get on my nerves. "Never give a damn" sometimes seemed to epitomize his way of relating.

But Bronc did give a damn, I reminded myself. He only acted like he didn't give a damn. That was the cowboy code of ethics.

"So why are you letting Tara get away with this?" I asked him.

"Why not? I got the horse back. Last thing I need is some damn cops in my hair. That's why I took you."

"Should I take it as a compliment that you prefer me to the cops?"

"You sure can if you want to." Bronc bared his teeth at me and I smiled back; normal behavior was restored.

As we rattled down the highway at a more or less sedate sixty, my mind shifted back to Tara. Tara who apparently had an alibi. But if I were Tara and I wanted to inherit, I'd arrange to split the money with some low-lifer and have him do the killing, then make sure I had an alibi. It all fit.

And Tara had a gun. The same sort of gun that had killed Jack. I wondered again if it had been one of a pair.

The trouble was that I wanted Tara to be guilty. Too much. If she had a motive, so did Jack's other two exes. And I had no idea what they were like or if they had alibis. All right, I told myself, there's a simple solution for this. By the time Bronc pulled back into the clinic parking lot and I climbed out of the truck, I'd made up my mind. I was going to meet wives number one and two.

SEVENTEEN

It turned out to be a relatively easy workday. I got through Jim's list of calls in record time, including one unscheduled emergency. Well, it wasn't really an emergency. The client just thought it was.

This particular client, a normally friendly, intelligent woman named Laurie Brown, was absolutely irrational on the subject of her horses. Something as minor as a small scrape was a full-blown disaster in her eyes. Today's emergency was just that one of her Peruvian Pasos had had a fairly standard reaction to the flu shot she'd given him yesterday, and was running a fever. It took me a good half-hour to reassure her that vaccine reactions like this were almost normal, and a couple of days on bute (horse aspirin) would take care of the problem.

Despite this minor glitch, it was only four o'clock and the thin winter sunlight still lay on the slopes of the mountains when I left the clinic. Another pretty day gone by. I rubbed Blue's head as I drove and he flattened his ears slightly in appreciation. His eyes looked sad, though—their habitual expression these days. Nothing I could do. Old age wasn't curable.

The urge to go to Lonny's and visit my horses was strong, but instead I took Bay Street and headed toward the ocean. Five minutes later I was driving into the little beachside town of Capitola. Capitola was charming with a capital C, the charm firmly decreed by the city council. The shops and restaurants were little and quaint and charming, the streets were narrow and curving and crowded and charming, the old houses were neatly painted and had charming flower gardens and window boxes. All this charm was enforced by the planning department with an iron hand, or so I heard.

I parked my truck in a large and uncharming municipal parking lot (the narrow streets were notoriously short of parking places), cracked the windows for Blue, and hiked half a mile to a steep stairway on an alley that led to a second-floor apartment over a boutique. My childhood friend Bret Boncantini was living here with his girlfriend, Deb. The apartment was actually Deb's. She paid the rent, and Bret merely lived with her, contributing, as far as I was aware, only his playful version of companionship.

I had no idea if Bret (or Deb) was home, but my luck was in. Bret's "Come on in" sounded in response to my knock, and I pushed the door open and walked into the one-room apartment. Bret was stretched out on a futon couch, watching a basketball game on TV, and he grinned when he saw me. "So what's up, Doc?"

"Not much." I cleared some magazines off a folding director's chair and sat down near him, glancing around at the blend of American innocuous and tropical exotic. Woven straw mats covered the dark brown shag carpet, South Seas batik fabrics draped a couple of conventional recliners, and Gauguin prints crowded palm-frond fans on the plain white walls. Every corner seemed to contain a large-leafed, overly lush green plant, and the whole effect was somehow quite reasonable and pleasant. I could, however, have done without the omnipresent TV set, which seemed to be riveting Bret's entire attention.

After his brief greeting his eyes had gone back to the screen

133

and remained firmly fixed there. I watched him watch it and smiled to myself. Some things never changed, and Bret seemed to be one of them.

He'd turn thirty this year, I happened to know, but you sure couldn't tell it by looking at him. His tanned skin, green-brown eyes and blond-streaked hair glowed undimmed; his expression was as carefree as it had ever been. Are you ever going to grow up? was a question many people felt inclined to ask Bret, and no, it appeared, he wasn't.

Feeling my gaze, Bret shifted his eyes from the TV to my face. There was a mischievous gleam in those eyes; it seemed to reside there permanently and was perhaps the secret behind Bret's legendary ability to fascinate women. I wouldn't know for sure. Bret and I had been friends for twenty-some years now, but we'd never been lovers. As far as I was concerned his playful irresponsibility made him good company—once in a while. How Deb managed to put up with him full-time I would never know.

"Do you know a woman named Elaine or Laney Hollister?" I asked him. "Jack Hollister's ex-wife. She's supposed to live in Capitola."

Bret was once more engrossed in the basketball game; he appeared not to hear my question. I repeated it louder.

Reluctantly he took his eyes off the tiny figures on the screen and looked at me. "Laney Hollister? Sure. Lives in that big house at the end of the street. That was too bad about old Jack, huh?" And back his attention went to the TV.

Well, that was lucky. I wasn't surprised that Bret knew Jack. Bret had made his living—or what living he made, anyway—for the last few years as a horseshoer. Thus he was familiar with most people in the horse business in Santa Cruz County. But it was a piece of luck I hadn't expected that he actually knew Jack's second ex. Of course, Bret had that amazing facility of seeming to know everybody.

"How do you know her?" I asked.

"Key West," he answered succinctly, his eyes on the game.

Key West was one of the little beachside bars Capitola was

known for. Lively, fashionable places, they were meccas for people who wanted a partner for the night—"meat market" bars.

"Elaine Hollister hangs out at Key West?" I asked Bret. Fortunately the television had moved on to a commercial, and I was able to capture his attention for a minute.

"Yep." He gave me the smile that had won a hundred hearts—crooked teeth, lit-up eyes. "She tried to take me home one night."

"And did you go?"

"Nope."

"Loyalty to Deb, I suppose."

Bret grinned again. "Partly. And old Elaine looks like trouble to me."

"Is she good-looking?" I asked, puzzled.

"Sure. For an older woman. But I like older women just fine."

"How old is she?"

"Fortyish, I guess. Fit-looking, blond, fancy—works out at the gym, still likes to show her figure off at the beach. She's a real local around here."

"So why does she look like trouble?"

"I dunno. But she does. After a while you can spot it. They've got this look in the eyes—strung a little too tight. Trying too hard. You just know this one would end up being a pain."

"Hmm." I wasn't sure what to make of this. Bret knew a lot about women, but his knowledge came from one point of view, so to speak. A woman who was "trouble" in his estimation might simply be one who wouldn't be likely to allow him to love her and leave her in the prompt way he usually preferred. On the other hand, I'd known Bret since we were children and his instincts were good. "Trouble" might also mean an unstable personality.

The basketball game was back on the screen and Bret's attention was once again riveted. I was about to give up and ask him to point out Elaine Hollister's house when his girlfriend walked in the door.

135

"Hi, Deb," I greeted her, feeling once again a sense of mild surprise that such a woman had chosen Bret.

Tall, red-headed, and beautifully proportioned, Deb was not conventionally pretty, but her face, all angles and bone, was both attractive and memorable. More than that, her green eyes were intelligent and her firm mouth humorous. I liked her tremendously, and couldn't imagine how Bret had gotten so lucky.

Her entrance got his mind off the game—at least for a minute. "Did you get any beer?"

"Yes."

He smiled at her. "Can't watch a basketball game without beer."

She set the bag of groceries she was carrying on the table, and I noticed Bret got up off the couch and went to fetch his own beer, appearing not to expect her to wait on him. Good sign.

"Would you like something, Gail? I've got some chardonnay in the refrigerator. Or there's a nice shiraz." Deb was always cordial.

I revised my thoughts of leaving. "I'll take the shiraz."

Deb got the bottle from the counter and poured two glasses. We shared a taste for good wine, though Deb knew a great deal more about it than I did. She worked as a waitress in the most elegant restaurant in Capitola, and had learned a good deal in the course of her job about both wine and food.

"So what are you up to?" she asked, as we settled ourselves on two wicker bar stools, our backs, in common unspoken opinion, to the TV.

"I'm trying to find out about a woman named Elaine Hollister," I said and took a sip of the shiraz. It was good, powerful and fruity at the same time.

"She lives at the end of the street," Deb said, "Did Bret tell you?"

"Uh-huh."

"What do you want to know about her? Does she need an alibi?"

I almost choked on a swallow of wine. Trying to cough and talk at the same time, I sputtered, "What do you mean?"

"Her ex-husband was murdered, right?"

"Yeah."

"So I wondered if she was a suspect and might need an alibi. And I know you, Gail." Deb grinned. "You're nosy."

I laughed. "Nosy" could quite accurately describe what I was doing.

"Anyway," Deb went on, "the reason I ask is I can give her an alibi."

"You're kidding."

"Nope. I was walking home from work that night, the night her ex was murdered, and I saw her walking to her front door right around midnight. Stumbling would be a better word."

"Was she drunk?"

"Blind. She was weaving down her front path and kind of came to rest on the door. I stood there for a minute, on the street, watching her, thinking she might need help, but she eventually got the key in the lock and staggered inside."

"Did she see you?"

"It's possible, but there's no way she would remember. She was way too drunk, not to mention that though I know her by sight, I doubt she would know me. She's the lady of the manor, we're just some of the peasants who live in the village." Deb said this without resentment, simply stating the facts of life.

I stared out the window toward a large three-story house on which Deb's eyes had been fixed while she told this story. "Is that her house?" I asked, pointing.

A last shaft of sunlight lit up the facade and front yard as Deb nodded an affirmative. "Yep."

The house was an extensively remodeled Victorian—so extensively, in fact, that there was very little Victorian character left to it. Someone had chosen to shingle it all over and preserve the shingles with a shiny golden-brown varnish. This, combined with an equally shiny forest-green trim, gave the house a vaguely nautical feeling that seemed to sit oddly with its steep old-fashioned roof and prominent bay window. The tiny front yard, immaculately landscaped, had that boring assortment of evergreen shrubs surrounding a handkerchief lawn that was the sure sign of some "professional" firm. It wasn't a homey-looking house. There was, however, a dark green Mercedes in the driveway.

I set my empty wineglass down and smiled at Deb. "I think I'm going to pay her a visit. Do you mind if I tell her you saw her that night?"

"No, that's fine. I'd be happy to tell my story to the cops."

"Thanks for the wine."

Deb murmured a good-bye; Bret barely nodded in my direction as I went quietly out the door, excited commentary from the TV trailing in my wake.

Laney Hollister's house seemed to tower above me as I walked up the front path. Three stories high, and wedged between its neighbors as city houses are, the steep pitch of its roof and the growing dusk made it seem even taller than it was. I banged the brass knocker on the shiny green front door and felt like a small, insignificant ant.

The woman who opened the door matched Bret's description. Roughly forty, she was still very pretty. And "pretty" was the word that came to mind. Her small, neat features had no drama or force, but they were appealing; equally so the trim figure, tanned skin, and long, wavy blond hair. It was the accoutrements, so to speak, that made my mouth drop open stupidly. In a second, I knew exactly what Bret meant by trouble.

Laney Hollister, for all her prettiness, looked ridiculous. She wore black jeans of an impossible tightness, clear plastic high-heeled sandals with rhinestones, a matching belt, and a black form-fitting knit top that bared her midriff and was deeply scooped to show her considerable cleavage. This top featured, unbelievably, a gold zipper with a large rhinestone-studded pull ring. To embellish this outfit she wore hot pink lipstick, chalky matte-tone foundation and blush, and eye shadow and mascara that looked like they'd been laid on with a trowel. Her scent was so heavy I had the impulse to take three fast steps backward. I stared at her in disbelief for a moment that verged on rudeness before I recovered my wits. "Ms. Hollister, I'm Dr. McCarthy. I was a friend of your ex-husband, Jack."

"Yes?" Her voice was high and chirpy, like a seventeen-year-old's. In fact, I realized, her whole getup and demeanor was that of a teenager; the wide-eyed look she gave me now had an innocent friendliness at strange variance with her cheap hooker appearance.

"Uh, this may sound kind of funny," I fumbled, "but a friend of mine happened to see you on the night Jack was murdered, and wondered if that might be of use to you."

Laney Hollister flapped her heavily mascaraed eyelashes up and down and then giggled. There was no other word for it. "Oh, you mean for an alibi?"

"Yes."

"Well, I was out with some friends that night so I already have one." She regarded me curiously. "I'm going out in a little while, but you could come in for a minute and tell me about it."

Since this was just what I'd been hoping for, I stepped promptly in the door, gazing around with frank interest that turned immediately to disappointment. The house, like the yard, had plainly been done by professionals. It wasn't unattractive, but it lacked any sort of individuality. Oriental rug copies lay on a polished oak floor with fake antiques in every corner. The many small china knickknacks and cute arrangements of dried flowers were right in scale with the rest of the junk.

I sat down on a plump cream-colored couch that faced the bay window, and smiled in my friendliest, most professional way at my hostess.

Laney Hollister looked uncomfortable. Fidgeting with a gold bracelet, she said, "You know, Dr., uh, McCarthy, I don't really think I need an alibi or anything. Nobody thinks I killed Jack."

I nodded encouragingly but didn't say anything, thinking of Jeri Ward's technique.

Laney sat in an armchair and crossed one leg over the other. "I'd be crazy to kill Jack. I mean, why would I?"

"For his money," I suggested. This was way out of line; I wondered how Laney would respond.

"Oh, you mean that silly will. Well, I wouldn't kill him for his money. That's ridiculous."

"You did know about his will, then?" I couldn't believe I was getting away with questioning her like this.

"Oh, I knew," she gave a brief pout. "We all knew."

"His other exes, you mean. Do you think one of them killed him?" Jesus, Gail, I thought in disgust. Why don't you just suggest Tara murdered the man.

Laney giggled again, apparently not bothered by the crude question. "I'd believe it. Especially Karen."

That wasn't what I'd had in mind. "Why Karen?" I asked.

"Karen's still very bitter, you know. She thinks I took Jack away from her, and then when Jack and I got divorced, she thought I got too much money. I think she really wants more money." Laney smiled sweetly.

"I thought Karen divorced Jack."

"Oh, she did. But it was because Jack and I were running around together and everybody knew it. Jack didn't try to hide it. He was in love with me." She said it proudly. I pictured her ten years or more ago, when the girlish manner wouldn't have contrasted so oddly with her age, and her looks would have been even more spectacular. I could understand a man being infatuated with her. A stupid man, anyway.

"What about Tara?" I asked, just to see how she'd react.

"Oh her." Laney sniffed. "I wouldn't know about her. I'm sure she needs money, too."

No love lost there, obviously. It was hard to picture the two women in the same room, they were such opposites. Other than being blond, good-looking, and dumb, I added.

Laney fidgeted a little in her chair and I realized my time was probably running out. Quickly I ran through Deb's story, leaving out, naturally, the dead-drunk aspect. Laney seemed neither concerned nor very interested, though she did decide to write down Deb's name and phone number. While she fetched paper and pen, I went rapidly through potential questions and settled on the most important one.

"Do you know where Karen lives?" I asked, wondering if this would be stretching even Laney's limits.

Apparently not. "Down on Beach Hill. In a condo. When she and Jack first separated, before I got married to him, I used to go drive by her place. It's weird, I know," she giggled, "but it's like I was so curious about her. I mean she hated me. It was strange. I'd drive by and look in her windows sometimes. I used to call her and hang up when she answered." Laney giggled again, clearly not bothered at revealing these somewhat embarrassing facts.

"Where on Beach Hill?" I asked, adding lamely, "I used to know Karen, years ago."

"On Cliff Street," she said. "Her condo's right on the corner of Cliff and Third. You can't miss it."

"Thanks," I said, handing her Deb's name and phone number, neatly printed on a sheet of notepaper that had a teddy bear in one corner and "Have a nice day" across the top.

"Sorry I have to rush you out." Laney led the way into her hall. "I'm going out to dinner and he should be here soon. I need to do my makeup."

I followed her, wondering exactly what she planned to add to the already impressive array of cosmetics on her face. Just how thick could you apply the stuff, anyway?

I was grinning to myself as she ushered me out, but the grin vanished instantly as I started down her walk. Someone was coming up it. Laney's dinner date? I looked again, not believing my eyes. The person coming up Laney's front walk was Travis Gunhart.

EIGHTEEN

It was almost dark, but Laney's porch light lit up Trav's aghast face reasonably clearly. We stared at each other with mutual expressions of horror; Laney looked nonplused.

"You're early," she said blankly, and I registered that she hadn't meant for me to see Travis.

He was wearing clean jeans, a pressed long-sleeved shirt, shiny cowboy boots, and a belt with a well-polished trophy buckle. His light brown hair was combed neatly and he definitely looked as "dressed for dinner" as I had ever seen him. He seemed half angry, half frightened, as the shock died out of his face. I had the brief impression that he thought of simply turning and running, realized it would be both ridiculous and useless, and chose to do the next best thing.

"Hi, Gail," he said curtly, and walked right by me. Brushing roughly past Laney, he stepped into her house.

Laney gave me an agitated look and followed him, shutting her shiny green front door behind her. I stood on her porch in a state of shock, staring at the green paint and brass knocker and drawing some very unwelcome conclusions.

Travis, my God. Travis was dating Laney. Or so it would

seem, anyway. Perhaps—the thought was even worse—he'd just teamed up with Laney to get a share of her inheritance. But Bronc had given Travis an alibi. I thought about that for a second. Would Bronc lie to protect Travis? Surely not if he thought Trav had murdered Jack?

But perhaps he thought Travis couldn't have done it and was simply protecting him by saying he'd been on the ranch when in fact he hadn't. And Bronc presumably didn't know Travis was seeing Laney.

I stared at the towering house, its colors dimmed to a uniform drabness by the progress of evening. Someone had drawn the curtains across the bay window. I shivered. It was getting cold and I was hungry. Not to mention I had no idea what to say if Travis came out.

Abruptly I started back toward my truck. I'd have dinner and think this through. Not that thinking would help. But I still had one more chore left to do. And, fortunately, I knew an excellent restaurant near Beach Hill.

Riva Fish House is right out on the Santa Cruz Wharf, over-looking Lighthouse Point and the Boardwalk. An almost full moon laid a silver-edged swath of ripples across the dark water of the bay as I drove down the old pier. Few people about, the carnival shapes of the Boardwalk still and ghostly in the off season, waves plashing against the pilings. A sharp little breeze lifted my hair off my face when I got out of the truck, and I took a deep breath of the cold, briny, winter-ocean smell.

Walking across the cracked tarmac, I pushed open Riva's swinging door and went inside. It's a pleasant place—windows looking out on the bay, recessed lighting, curving stainless-steel trim complementing a polished mahogany bar. Most important, it has that indefinable something a bar needs to have—a rest-fulness even when crowded with chattering tourists. Tonight the throngs were absent, and I ordered a glass of zin from an attentive bartender and stared absently at my reflection in the mirror as I sipped it.

143

Shit. I still couldn't believe what I'd just seen. Travis was involved, in some sense, with one of Jack's exes. It almost seemed like incest. Worse, it gave Travis a hell of a good reason for murdering Jack.

Damn. Somehow cuss words were all that seemed to come to mind. I took another sip of zin and wondered what to do next. Well, obviously have dinner. And then visit Karen Harding, I supposed. Though talking to Karen suddenly seemed a whole lot less important. But I'd come this far, I told myself; I wasn't quitting until I'd met the last player in this cast of characters.

Taking another swallow of wine, I looked my reflection straight in the eye. The Gail in the bar mirror looked tired and disheveled—a typical end-of-the-day look. Rough strands of hair that had escaped my ponytail hung about my face. I didn't look like a successful, competent veterinarian; in fact, I looked a bare level of decency above a street person. And I certainly did not look, or feel, ready for another stressful encounter.

But a good dinner will fix a lot of things. I got a table with a perfect view of the moonlit bay and Lighthouse Point—the little toy of a lighthouse seeming a childish frivolity—pretty but useless on such a brilliant night. I ordered scallops Provençal, some sourdough bread, and another glass of zin, and started to feel better.

By the time I was done eating I felt fine. I'd even organized my approach to Karen Harding, who couldn't possibly be as soft a touch as Laney had been. Taking a few minutes in the bathroom, I combed my hair, washed my face, and practiced my professional smile. Not bad.

As I drove toward Beach Hill I put an arm around Blue and rubbed his chest as he leaned into me. "I know, I know," I told him, "you want to go home. This is the last stop, I promise."

Blue flattened his ears mildly when I parked the truck—the Cliff House condos were obvious, as Laney had said—and I rubbed his wedge-shaped head a minute as I stared out the window. The group of condos soared into the air, tall and sleek and modern, with many terraces and balconies on the upper stories that looked as though they would have good views of the bay. In the moonlight, the place appeared to be painted gray and white, but that could have been an illusion. I got out of the truck and locked it, then walked to the bank of mailboxes. "Harding" was printed plainly next to number three. This woman, unlike Jack's other exes, had chosen to use her maiden name. And, by Laney's account anyway, she was still bitter about the divorce. I wondered if that had any significance. Surely you didn't murder someone twenty years after a divorce out of residual bitterness? But for money, I thought, maybe.

Condo number three was right on the corner, just as Laney had told me. I knocked firmly on the door and waited. In a minute I heard the sound of the peephole sliding open. I tried to look bland. A moment later the door opened a few inches, still on the chain. A woman peered out the crack. "Yes?"

She was heavy, and had short curly gray hair. She wore purple polyester pants and a lavender sweatshirt with a kitten on the front, but nothing could have been less cuddly than her expression. Harsh lines scored her face from nose to mouth and ran across her forehead; looking at the cigarette in her hand, I knew part of the reason. The eyes that looked out at me told the rest of the story; they were suspicious and wary, on the edge of hostility.

I smiled at her. "I'm Dr. Gail McCarthy. I was a friend of your ex-husband, Jack."

She listened without any response, facial or verbal, and I wondered if she heard what I was saying. I went doggedly on. "I was up at the veterinary convention and I had a conversation with him the day before he was murdered, in which he mentioned you and some money he was planning to give you. I haven't told the police about this, and I thought I'd talk to you first."

"I have nothing to hide from the police," she said flatly, but she didn't shut the door.

"Can I come in?" I asked.

She thought about this. "Do you have any identification?" she said at last.

"My driver's license and a business card," I told her. "Would you like to see them?"

"Yes."

I fished the small wallet out of the back pocket of my jeans, showing her my license and handing her a card. She stared at this for several long moments before she took the chain off the hook and opened the door. "I guess you can come in."

Following her into her living room, I looked around with my usual curiosity, but this room was as characterless as Laney's house had been, though a little less cute. The furniture was routine department-store stuff, the carpet, drapes, and walls in shades of gray and white. The only personal touch was the dozens of framed photographs—on the mantel, on the end tables, a few on the walls. One large, ornately framed example over the fake fireplace showed an unfamiliar landscape of rolling hills lit with low light, two horsemen in the foreground, both wearing cowboy hats and Western gear.

"That's a nice photo," I said.

"My father and brother. On our family ranch in Merced."

"Oh."

Bronc had said Karen came from a ranch family, I remembered. It seemed sad that she'd ended up in this sterile condo.

Karen sat down on her couch, facing a still noisy TV set; I took a seat in a gray velour recliner and thought I knew why she'd decided to let me in. A tumbler of amber liquid with ice cubes in it sat on the coffee table in front of the couch; next to it was a very full ashtray. Not a foot away, perched on a stack of *Ladies' Home Journals,* was a picked-over frozen dinner. Karen's eyes, as she looked at me, showed a flicker of avid interest underlying the wariness, which I suspected was more habitual than personally directed against me. I'd clearly interrupted a boring evening. Perhaps—grim thought—all her evenings were like this. No wonder she was bitter.

I cleared my throat, trying to think of a graceful way to lead into my phony story, and my eye was caught by a framed eight-by-ten photograph on the table next to me. It showed a young woman standing in front of a ranch house—the Hollister Ranch house, I realized with a jolt. The woman had long blond hair tied back in a ponytail and a youthful, shiny-eyed prettiness. The white dress was sashed at the waist and accentuated her prominent curves.

"Is that you?" I asked, trying to hide my surprise.

She laughed, a rough smoker's laugh, a sound without any humor or warmth. "I didn't always look like this, you know."

"I'm sorry," I said awkwardly. "I didn't mean to be rude." It's just, I added silently, that I hadn't realized Karen had been another pretty, curvy blonde. Jack, I now saw, had been very predictable.

"About this money," I began, not having any better ideas on how to lead into it smoothly, "I didn't want to put you in an uncomfortable position by talking to the police before I talked to you."

Karen shrugged. "Tell the police. I don't know what you're talking about anyway."

"Jack said he was going to give you some money," I said tentatively.

"Well, he owed it to me," she spat, a sudden flash of anger breaking through her reserve. Considering, she took a long drag on her cigarette and went on more calmly, "I didn't get anything out of the divorce. I can't even afford to buy a decent house. Jack owed me."

"You'll have plenty now," I said experimentally.

Karen laughed again—not a pleasant sound. "Are you implying I killed him to get it?"

"Well no, of course not."

She puffed some more on her cigarette and looked away. "Just what are you here for, then?"

"I thought I should talk to you first . . ." I began.

"You said that already." She coughed and looked at me sharply. "What's your interest?"

147

Having finagled my way in the door, I saw no harm in telling the truth. "My friend was out with Jack the night he was murdered. I introduced them, so I got questioned. I sort of got drug into the whole thing."

"So you're not Jack's latest floozy?"

"No."

She gave the harsh laugh. "I wondered. You're not his type."

That was true enough. Not blond, only average-sized tits, and, hopefully, a whole lot smarter.

"Have the police asked you for an alibi for the night of Jack's murder?" I asked her, wondering how far I'd get.

Apparently, I'd pushed too hard. Her face became hostile and suspicious; the brief window of curiosity snapped shut. "It's none of your business." She bit the words off. "You're not a reporter or a private detective or something, are you?"

"No, I'm a vet, like I told you."

"Well, no one thinks I killed Jack. And you'd better not be saying I did."

Her interest in me was dead. Her eyes went to the TV, which had been dinning mercilessly in our ears the whole time, some sitcom with bursts of frenetic conversation and blasts of canned laughter. I decided to make my exit before I was asked to. Karen's profile, angry and dissatisfied, didn't bode well for more cozy chatting.

"Thanks for your time," I said as I stood up.

She grunted or mumbled some response, not audible to me, and followed me to her front door. As she unbolted it, I stared at the nearest framed eight-by-ten on the wall in front of me. A closeup of three women, one of them recognizably Karen Harding, looking much as she did right now. The second woman was more or less the same age and very similar-looking. A sister? The third woman was younger—in her twenties—blond, pretty, uncannily familiar.

Karen had the door open. "Go on. I've had enough of your snooping around."

I stepped over the doorstep, started to turn around and heard

148

the door slamming behind me. Our interview was definitely at an end. But that picture . . .

I walked to the truck and unlocked it, wrapped in my own fog. The younger woman in the picture looked like the young Karen. A Karen with short, blond hair. But . . .

It couldn't be, I told myself. It simply couldn't be. But I had to know. I started the truck and pulled out, reaching for the car phone as I did so, hoping I could remember the number.

It took several rings, but eventually a familiar voice said, "Hello?"

I couldn't think of a graceful way to do it. "Joanna, do you know someone named Karen Harding?"

Silence.

"This is Gail," I said at last.

"I know."

"Joanna, you'd better tell me," I said slowly. "I can find out, one way or another."

More silence.

"If I can find out, so can the cops. Joanna, is Karen related to you?"

"She's my aunt." Her voice was barely audible. "The reason I recognized Jack there in the coffee shop was that I'd seen pictures of him, that my mother had. I didn't want it to come up."

"Don't be stupid," I begged her. "It's bound to come out eventually. Why didn't you tell me? You didn't tell that detective either, did you?"

"Of course not. How do you think it would look to him? Here I am, without an extra nickel, and it turns out my aunt is going to inherit a lot of money when Jack died. And I happened to go out with him the night he was killed?"

"You knew Karen would inherit?"

"My mother told me that, years ago. She said Karen couldn't wait for the promiscuous son-of-a-bitch to kick the bucket."

"Did Jack know who you were when you went out with him?"

"No. He had no idea."

"Are you sure?"

149

"He never said anything, if he did."

"Have you been in touch with Karen?"

"No. I haven't talked to her in months. Like I told you, I didn't want the whole thing to come up."

We were both quiet. I had no idea what to say, or even what to think. Joanna finally broke the silence. "I don't need any more stress in my life right now, Gail." She was almost pleading. "I'm trying to get over Todd and put my life together again, and I just want to be let alone to do it. All right?"

"I don't think it can happen like that," I said. "I think you need to talk to the cops and get this cleared up before they come looking for you."

"Well, I'm not going to. And if you're any kind of a friend at all, you won't tell them either."

Oh shit. Now she was mad. But there was one more thing I had to know. "Joanna, Karen didn't promise you any money after Jack died, did she?"

"Of course she didn't. I can't believe you said that." And Joanna hung up.

I listened to the buzz on the airwaves for a while, then slowly put the receiver back in its cradle. My thoughts were disconnected, drifting like thistledown on the wind. I made the turn onto Old San Jose Road without really seeing it and headed up the hill toward home.

Redwoods slipped by outside the truck windows; moonlight illuminated the rounded shoulders of the hills. I felt lost. I thought I knew Joanna, and yet did I? Did I know anyone, really?

Pulling into my driveway, I unlocked my front door, letting Blue and an instantly appearing Bonner inside. I thought about Karen, Laney, and Tara as I fed the two animals. Three women—so superficially different, so essentially alike. As I pulled off my clothes and wiggled gratefully between my flannel sheets, the one inescapable thought in my mind was that maybe Jack Hollister had been a lot different than I'd supposed.

I tried to postulate a new Jack, one who only noticed a woman's looks, never her attitude, who had been more lucky and ambitious than smart. A closed-minded, oblivious man with a petty, vindictive streak. A man who had decided to run a new vet out of town because he perceived him as competition.

Having got this harsh portrait more or less in place I tried to refine the repercussions in the light of Jack's subsequent murder. The only thing that came to mind was the notion that this Jack was more likely to have incurred enmity than the easygoing rancher I'd thought I knew. But there would have to have been a reason to murder him. People are not killed, at least I didn't think so, simply because they're abrasive. And what it still came down to was that the three ex-wives had the motive.

On top of which, Joanna was related to wife number one. But, I reminded myself, the cops had concluded that the gun wouldn't have fit in Joanna's purse. She was innocent, surely.

But there was no getting around the next one. Travis Gunhart was involved with wife number two. Travis had Bronc for an alibi, but Bronc had seemed strangely disturbed about Trav. Was that because he was aware that Travis had been gone that night?

I wiggled my head deeper into the pillow and sighed. I'd always liked Trav. He had seemed such a happy, outgoing kid, with an open-hearted manner that was very appealing. In some ways, he reminded me of Bret. But Trav was no ladykiller. He wasn't attractive in that intense, visceral way that seems to draw females like moths—a trait I'd noticed Bret had to the nth degree. Trav was just nice and talkative and willing to be friends— which made his affair with Laney, if in fact it was an affair, seem all the more calculated.

She could have picked him up at a bar like she tried to do with Bret, I reminded myself. He might not have known she was Jack's ex-wife. Now there was an interesting question. Had Travis been working for Jack when Jack was married to Laney? When exactly had Travis started living and working on the Hollister Ranch? Where had he come from and why had he ended up there, more or less permanently? I didn't know the answers to any of these questions.

And Trav had seemed very different since Jack's murder. I'd thought that it might have been grief, but now what did I think?

I groaned into the pillow. I didn't know what I thought, but I couldn't stomach the idea that Travis had killed Jack.

Tara? Tara had an alibi, verifiable by four or five people. If Tara was the killer, I would have to find out who she had bought off or hired. That was the cops' job, I reminded myself, and I hoped they were doing it.

Who else might have a motive? Maybe, I thought suddenly, the money to be gained through Jack's death wasn't inherited. Joanna had said that Jack talked to her about some big land deal that could make him a lot of money. Maybe this business deal would stand or fall based on Jack's removal from the scene. Maybe someone else would win or lose a fortune.

I sure as shit didn't have a clue who that person might be. Still, I knew Jack's real estate agent. She was a horsewoman, naturally, and when Jack had more or less retired, she'd begun using me as her vet. I could at least ask her if she knew about Jack's upcoming deal and try to figure out who it would benefit or harm.

Always supposing, that was, that the obvious didn't happen and Jeri Ward didn't promptly arrest Laney and Trav. Or Tara. Or Joanna.

Oh Lord. I turned firmly over in the bed, shoved my face into the pillow, and tried hard to forget the whole situation. God, I was glad I wasn't a cop.

NINETEEN

I was fast asleep when they came knocking on the door. I was aware at first only that something was wrong, then of loud, noisy banging, then I was awake and someone was pounding on my front door at well past eleven o'clock. Blue barked raspily from his spot by the bed—an old dog's bark, but still vigorous. What the hell? I wasn't on call this week, so that couldn't be it, even allowing for the absurd notion that a frantic client would come banging on my door in the middle of the night.

"Who is it?" I shouted, as loudly as I could.

Since my house is built on two levels, with the bedroom on the lower story and the front door upstairs at street level, the knocker could probably barely hear me. Especially over Blue's barking.

Eventually I made out a return shout, which sounded alarmingly like "Police!"

Climbing out of bed, I sifted through the discarded clothes on the floor; I could hardly appear for the police in my underwear. Jeans and a sweatshirt rendering me decent, I told Blue firmly to stay there and shut up, and climbed my ladder to the upper story.

"Who is it?" I demanded again, once I was upstairs.

The cool voice on the other side of the door was unmistakable. "This is Detective Jeri Ward of the Santa Cruz County Sheriff's Department."

"Okay," I muttered, unbolting the door with one hand and turning on the light with the other.

There were two of them on my porch when I got the door open and stood blinking stupidly out, my eyes dazzled by the sudden blast of light. Jeri Ward, dignified in a suit of olive wool with pumps, nylons, the whole works, and Claude Holmquist, every bit as formal in an iron gray suit with a dark red tie. I registered these details one by one as I stood there staring in the blank fashion of someone who was snoring soundly one minute before.

"Can we come in?" Jeri Ward asked finally.

"I guess so." Gracelessly, I moved aside and went to sit on the end of the couch.

The two detectives entered the room in the cautious manner of people who are used to unexpected trouble, their eyes taking in the surroundings with quick, careful, impersonal glances. Huddled in my corner of the couch, I felt their rigid presence skewing my comfortable environment into messy chaos.

Suddenly I was aware of the crooked stacks of books on the antique dresser, the fuzzy layer of dog hair on the wingback chair where Jeri Ward was gingerly sitting down. After a distrustful glance at the only other chair, an admittedly rickety-looking rocker, Claude Holmquist seated himself at the far end of the couch, which was, like the chairs and carpet, supporting a fair amount of Blue's excess coat. No doubt, I thought, torn between embarrassment and amusement, a flea would hop onto his nice gray suit. It would be the crowning touch.

Nobody was saying anything, and I wasn't going to be the one to break the silence. I stared at the three of us, reflected in the mirror over my antique dresser: Jeri Ward looked stiff, Claude Holmquist looked bland, I looked rumpled and sleepy, but all of our expressions were guarded.

Jeri began. "We've been to visit Karen Harding, Gail. Apparently we just missed you."

Her unexpected use of my first name, and the quasi-friendly tone in which she spoke startled me. A second's reflection dissected the tone into exasperation overlaid with sarcasm. I could feel my face shutting down even farther.

Detective Ward went on. "I have to warn you, you cannot go on doing this. You're not a cop, you're not even a PI. We are not going to have some civilian amateur sleuth mucking up a homicide investigation."

Anger flashed in me and I opened my mouth, but she held up a hand. "I know. You have helped us out before. But you need to understand that for me to have you going around questioning suspects and tainting their evidence is the same as if you were operating on a horse in order to save its life and I insisted on sticking my hand in its guts and fumbling around."

That shut me up. Was that what I was—a colossal, possibly life-endangering, pain in the ass? Maybe. But I had helped her out before. And what had happened to the rapport between us? Had it been swallowed by her need to play up to this Nevada cop? Was she so busy being defensive about her position vis-à-vis him that she'd simply forgotten the times when she hadn't considered me a pain?

Her face gave no clue; it was as controlled as ever. For a second I wondered just how she managed to stay so unmussed and unflappable at what must have been the end of a long day—and then I shifted my eyes to Detective Holmquist.

Predictably, he was watching me, that gentle, mild-seeming gaze fixed on my face. "Did you learn anything from Ms. Harding?"

Startled once again, I stared at him, trying to decide what traps this new approach held. Taking a page out of the bureaucratic book, I asked, "Why are you asking me?"

"To see if you can help us," he replied promptly. "I understand Detective Ward's problem with your involvement, but since you are already involved, it seems, I'd like to share your information."

All this was said with his eyes on my face; he never once looked at Jeri Ward. He's one-upping her, I thought. He's telling her, ever so subtly, that it's his case, he's the senior officer; he's backing her off. Instantaneously I revised this idea. Maybe they were just playing bad cop/good cop. Maybe the whole thing was prearranged.

Either way, I had nothing to lose by telling him what little I knew about Karen. Running my fingers through the messy tangle of my bangs, I thought about it. "I didn't actually learn much," I said, adding mentally that Karen, like Tara and Laney, used to be curvy and blond, and certainly seemed dumb.

"She appeared to be pretty bitter about Jack and said he 'owed' her. Said she didn't get enough money out of the divorce. I don't know if you'd call that a motive for murder. I was wondering if she had an alibi?" I ended on a questioning note, curious as to what he'd do with this.

I could feel Jeri Ward's eyes drilling into the side of my head, but I kept my own gaze fixed firmly on Detective Holmquist. If they were going to play good cop/bad cop, I might as well talk to the one with the sympathetic role.

I had, once again, underestimated the man. He never missed a beat. Cooperation was the name of his game, it appeared, and unhesitatingly he told me. "She has an alibi, more or less. She was seen by her neighbor at five P.M., picking up her newspaper, and this same neighbor reports that her car remained in the carport until she, the neighbor, went to bed. The neighbor said that Ms. Harding's routine was exactly the same every evening and it didn't vary on the night in question. Apparently those condos have pretty thin walls, and the neighbor could hear her moving around the kitchen and living room, and later—about eleven or so—going up the stairs to the bedroom."

"I guess that's an alibi." I said it without thinking, aware only after I spoke that the words—and more, the tone—revealed my continued interest in this case. Before Jeri Ward could snap a putdown, I asked Claude Holmquist, "What land deal was Jack involved in?"

He regarded me quietly, his normal mask of bland neutrality slipping a little so that I glimpsed the hard-edged mind within. I wondered what he was thinking.

Jeri Ward cut firmly across his thoughts, whatever they were. "Do you have any idea who might have killed him?" Back to the bad cop. "No," I said bluntly.

"Was he sexually involved with anyone?" Jeri fired the questions at me like tennis balls.

"I wouldn't know," I shot back. After a second, I added, "I saw him with a lot of different women over the last year. No one I knew, and they were always changing. I don't know who, if anyone, he'd been seeing lately."

"Was he involved with drugs?" Jeri's tone didn't change when she asked this question, but, once again, I was shocked.

"Jack? Jack was the last man on earth to be involved with drugs. At least," I paused, "I wouldn't have thought so." Again it occurred to me how little I really knew Jack Hollister. "Do you have some reason to suppose he used drugs?" I asked, thinking of Tara, and Lonny's sense that she had a "habit."

"Just answer the question," Jeri Ward snapped at me, but Detective Holmquist's quiet voice intervened.

"Let's all take it easy." To me, he added, "It's a standard line of questioning. First we concentrate on the immediate family of the victim, and anyone who stands to benefit directly by his or her death. In this case, the ex-wives. If these suspects are alibied out, which they seem to be here, we look around for other motives. Sexual involvement, involvement with drugs—these are key areas."

I nodded, looking at him, avoiding Jeri. "I have no reason to think Jack was involved with drugs," I said carefully. "There is some question about Tara."

At this, both detectives seemed to focus in. Claude Holmquist took out a small notepad and a pen and scribbled briefly. Jeri Ward said sharply, "Could you explain that statement, please?"

I lost my temper. I suppose I felt guilty for bringing it up at all. Whatever the reason, I laid my ears back and lashed out at her. "What the hell is your problem? You come barging in here, wake me up, want to pick my brain, and you're being goddamn rude to me. Where do you get off? Is there some kind of law against my talking to these people? I don't get your attitude at all."

"Yes, there is a law," Jeri said evenly. "I can put you in jail for obstructing a homicide investigation."

We stared at each other. I knew my own eyes were hot and angry; hers looked cold and hard. "So put me in jail," I snapped.

For a second I thought I'd provoked her too far; I saw a blast of some strong emotion rip across that taut face. "Don't try me too hard, Gail. You're interfering in something you've no business to be involved in. You're not helping anybody here. It's your duty to assist us, and you'd better be forthcoming with what it is you know about Tara Hollister and drugs, or I may just slap you in jail."

"Now, now, wait a minute here." Detective Holmquist raised his hand firmly, quelling any ill-judged reply I might have made. "I think we all have the same goal, don't we? We want this murderer arrested. So, Gail, can you tell me anything about Tara Hollister that connects her to drug use?"

Frowning, I stomped on my emotions and tried to choose my words carefully. "I don't know that Tara used drugs. What I know, more or less, is she ran through a lot of money in two years and doesn't appear to have any left. There's been gossip about her doing drugs, and she hangs out with people who have been said to use drugs. And it's a way to go through a lot of money." I thought about what I'd just said and added, "I don't like Tara. You should probably know that, too."

I wondered if I should tell them about Tara stealing Willy and decided not. That was really Bronc's business. And I couldn't see what possible bearing it could have on Jack's murder. Just like the fact that Tara had ridden JD to death and sued his former owner—these things illuminated what a nasty piece of work the woman was, that was all.

Detective Holmquist caught my hesitation and prodded gently. "Anything else you can tell us?"

There sure as shit was, I thought grimly. That Travis was seeing Lancy would doubtless seem as pertinent to them as it did to me. Not to mention the fact that Joanna was Karen's niece. But I shut my mouth firmly and shook my head. Damned if I was going to hand them anything. They hadn't endeared themselves to me. I could always tell them later, I reassured myself.

Instead, I said blandly, "Do you suppose one of the ex-wives might have hired a professional to do it? Offered to split her inheritance?"

Claude Holmquist made another note on his pad and said, "We've considered that, of course. A twenty-two is frequently the weapon of choice for a professional. The fact that the serial numbers were filed off points in that direction, too."

"But no evidence so far?"

"No, no evidence so far."

We are all quiet. I was aware, suddenly, of how tired I was. Today had been a long day. I stood up. "Look, I need to go back to bed. I have to go to work tomorrow. If I can help you any more, just let me know."

Detective Holmquist stood up, too, and Jeri Ward followed suit. I knew, as I followed them to the door, that some sort of parting shot was bound to be coming. Claude Holmquist contented himself with "Good night, Dr. McCarthy," but Jeri Ward stopped and faced me. "I mean it, Gail. You can't be questioning murder suspects. You're putting yourself in danger and hindering the investigation. I want your word you'll stop."

"Fine," I said wearily. "I'll stop. Good luck with the investigation."

"Thank you." She looked as cool as ever as I shut the door behind her.

TWENTY

So how illegal, immoral, and downright wrong is it to lie to the cops? This was the question that was occupying my mind at seven o'clock the next morning as I drove to work. I'd said I'd stay out of the investigation, but I either had to tell the detectives about Travis and Laney and Karen and Joanna or look into it myself.

Dammit, Gail, tell the cops and be done with it. That was the voice of reason. But there was another small voice that would not shut up. What about Travis, what will this do to him? And Joanna, whose life was in turmoil already? What makes you think the cops will handle this well, it said.

I couldn't get that last idea out of my head. I simply have no great faith in government enterprises, in bureaucratic organizations of any sort. I often think they are at least as likely, if not more likely, to get things wrong as to get them right.

I dithered all the way to work, but my mind was jerked sharply off the subject of Jack's murder when I walked into the office. Jim was the only one there and he was talking on the phone, but he crooked a finger at me and handed me a piece of paper. It was the results of the blood tests I'd run on Rebby. The lab work said he was positive for EPM.

Oh shit. This was one message I was going to have to deliver personally. Before Jim could get off the phone and tell me I had to do something else, I was out of the office and in my truck.

I drove to Kris's feeling apprehensive; what I saw when I pulled into her barnyard didn't alleviate my fears any. Kris was leaning on the corral fence, staring fixedly at her horse as he staggered around his pen. Even from the truck, I could see that his strange way of moving had not improved.

Getting out of the cab, I walked over to stand next to Kris. She didn't say a word, just kept watching Rebby. The slump of her shoulders and the droop of her head reminded me forcibly of Joanna—Joanna during those two miserable days in Tahoe.

It had to be said. I put my hand on her shoulder. "He tested positive for EPM."

Kris started crying. She tried to hide it by looking away from me and surreptitiously passing her sleeve across her face, but I knew.

It was Joanna all over again. And I still didn't know what to do. I wondered suddenly if I was missing some sort of emotional capacity that was necessary for female bonding. An even more unwelcome thought followed. Perhaps I was so vested in being in control of my world—a feeling that had grown out of my parents' early death—that I was drawn to women like Joanna and Kris because they seemed entirely competent and in charge. They made me feel safe. And when they lost that quality, when they seemed frightened and vulnerable, I withdrew—afraid of their vulnerability, which was too much like my own hidden fears.

Shit. It was certainly the ultimate in emotional withdrawal to be sitting here psychoanalyzing myself while Kris was in dire need of comfort. Enfolding her in a sisterly hug was probably what I ought to be doing, but it just wasn't me. I wasn't sure it was Kris, either.

As I stood there next to her, Reb waddled awkwardly from his water trough to his feeder and began eating. Jesus, I thought, why did it have to happen to him? Followed immediately by, At

161

least it wasn't Plumber or Gunner, thank God. And then I was ashamed.

I put my hand on Kris's shoulder. "I'm sorry," I said. "I don't know what to tell you. Wait and see is hard to do, I know, but I guess it's all we've got. Feed him his medication and watch him. The literature on this says it can take up to six weeks to see a response."

"Maybe he won't get better." Kris said quietly. "Then what?"

I shook my head and shrugged helplessly. "You'll have to decide. Is his quality of life good enough? Do you want to keep a crippled horse for a pet? Is he happy? Things like that." I added hastily, "We're not there yet, Kris, don't give up."

"I'm not," she said, but she sounded as forlorn and defeated as a little kid lost in a shopping mall.

I kept my hand on her shoulder. I knew how she felt, how I would feel in her position. Her baby was hurt and she couldn't help him.

"He's been such a great horse, Gail; he's done everything for me." Kris swallowed hard on a sob.

I patted her arm. This was the downside to being a veterinarian, these cases where you feel you've failed, or are failing. The times when you can't alleviate the suffering, can't fix the animal, can't restore the grieving person's world to wholeness— these are the cases that keep you awake at night.

As if on cue, Reb lifted his head from his feed and gently bumped my elbow with his nose. I rubbed his forehead with its white star and felt tears start to rise in my own eyes. This was such a nice horse.

Firmly, I squelched the emotion, gritting my teeth hard together, compressing my lips. I would not cry. It wasn't going to help Kris if I broke down.

Instead, when I thought I had everything under control, I said, I hoped cheerfully, "Let's look on the bright side. A lot of horses make amazing recoveries on this medication."

Kris nodded dully.

I squeezed her shoulder. "Hang in there. Call me anytime. I don't know exactly what I can do, but I'll sure come."

She nodded again and said a brief thanks, but she kept her eyes on Reb.

"Well, see you later then." I climbed back into my truck feeling useless and stupid. Blue, always in touch with my emotions, laid his chin on my thigh and stared worriedly up at me. I rubbed his head as I drove down Kris's driveway, thinking frustrated thoughts.

Rebby's case was just like Jack's murder and the investigation that followed it; there simply were no easy answers. And in both cases I desperately wanted a solution. I wanted to fix the problem. It's my nature, I guess. It's why I'm a vet.

Groaning out loud, I reached for the truck phone. I called the office and was informed that, like yesterday, the schedule was light, which was somewhat typical for midwinter. Jim had taken all the regular calls; the only thing for me was a colic case, a mild one, the client had said. Denise Hennessy's place.

I almost dropped the phone. "Denise Hennessy?"

The receptionist started to give me directions, but I cut her off. "No, no, I'm sorry, I know where it is. I was just thinking of something else."

I hung up the phone, hardly believing my luck, if that's what you want to call it. Denise Hennessy was, had been, Jack Hollister's real estate agent.

I knew where she lived—not far from Lonny, in the Aptos hills. It was a ten-minute drive, and I used the entire ten minutes wondering what, if anything, to ask her. By the time I drove into her graveled barnyard, I'd almost forgotten what I was there for.

Staring out my truck windshield I could see a horse staring back at me over the corral fence, his ears forward in lively interest. He nickered—a deep huh, huh, huh sound—when I got out of the pickup.

A sick horse does not look at you with his ears up, as bright and bushy-tailed as a baby fox. This guy was a common enough

Quarter Horse–type gelding in appearance, brownish bay with some white on his forehead and one leg, distinguished only by the wide-eyed intelligence on his face. His expression alone branded him as both healthy (for the moment, anyway) and a likable character.

"Hi, fella," I said, as I walked in his direction.

"Hey, Gail," came from off to my right. Denise had been sitting on a haystack in a small pole barn, half hidden by the shadow of the shed roof. She was climbing down now, talking as she walked to meet me. "I know, I know, he looks fine. I swear he was colicked an hour ago."

I smiled. "They do that. This isn't the first time it's happened. Better than if he was worse, anyway."

Denise smiled back and kept chattering—when the horse had first gone down, when he had rolled, how long she had walked him. Nervousness increased her natural loquacity and her pleasantly musical voice seemed to rush over me in a torrent of lightly accented vowels and rolling consonants.

Denise Hennessy was about my own age and had come from Ireland with her parents as a teenager; her lilting Irish accent was still very pronounced. I loved the sound of her voice, and could listen to her for hours, which was a good thing, as she loved to talk. Calls to Denise's place tended to be longer than scheduled.

I interrupted her recitation now by saying, "Why don't you catch him and I'll check him out."

She took a halter from a peg in the shed and went into the corral, still talking nonstop. I watched her, thinking that stereotypes and clichés became such because they were often so very true. Denise was too Irish to be real, with her bubbly, laughing talk, her triangular face, curly black hair, green eyes, generous freckles. She was talking to her horse now, as she caught him, and was still alternately commiserating with him and describing his condition to me as she led him out of the corral.

I took his pulse and respiration, checked his temperature, listened to his gut sounds—everything seemed normal. By

Denise's account he had showed mild colic symptoms an hour ago, the symptoms lasting about twenty minutes, then disappearing. I recommended to her that we give him a shot of painkiller, just to be on the safe side—this sort of colic was notorious for recurring just as the vet drove out of the barnyard—and that she watch him closely for the next twelve hours. She was content with this, holding the horse while I injected eleven cc's of banamine into his jugular vein.

When we were done and she was turning the gelding back out into his pen, I said, "You were Jack Hollister's real estate agent, weren't you?"

As I'd more than half expected, this simple little question unleashed a lively monologue. Yes, she'd been his agent, she'd known him forever, wasn't it terrible . . . etc. Eventually this petered out, though, with no information about current land deals included. I was forced to prod.

"Were you working on anything for Jack when he was killed?" And Jeri Ward would kill you for that one, I told myself, but, hell, it was just too tempting.

Denise's green eyes narrowed and she glanced at me shrewdly; for all her friendly blather, she was far from dumb. "And just why are you wanting to know?" The singsong accent and quick smile took the sting out of her words. Still, I was aware she'd meant them.

"My friend Joanna's a suspect, sort of." I told a much abridged story of Joanna and her report that Jack had talked of an upcoming deal. Denise listened closely, head cocked a little to one side.

"Well, I can be telling you, I suppose. Just don't pass it along. Jack was in escrow on a ranch."

"But which ranch?" I asked her. "Jack had ranches all over the western United States."

"Oh, I didn't do Jack's out-of-town work," Denise said in obvious surprise. "He had other people for that. But I did his local stuff. He bought several pieces of land around here, you know, and then sold them to developers."

"So which ranch was he selling?"

"The old ranch. The Hollister Ranch, it's called."

"Not the Hollister Ranch. It couldn't be." This time it was my turn to look and sound surprised.

"Well, I don't know about that. He was certainly in escrow. And Redwoods Inc., that's the developers, aren't happy at all right now. It'll be years, I'm sure, before the whole thing's straightened out. There goes my commission," she added philosophically.

"You're sure it was the Hollister Ranch," I said, oblivious to her commission and other issues, following a track of my own.

"Sure I'm sure."

"And the deal was going to go through?"

"Oh yes. It was solid. Jack would have had a lot of money coming in this week, if he'd lived."

"Oh," I said blankly.

Taking a quick leave of Denise, with a promise to come back promptly if her horse got worse, I climbed into my pickup with my head full of convoluted connections. The farther I drove the more complicated they got, until I patted the seat in an invitation to Blue. Stiffly he climbed up beside me and leaned into my body; I put my arm around him and rubbed him. Eventually I sighed, which caused him to turn his head and lick my cheek.

"Nothing makes any sense," I told him. "Nothing at all."

TWENTY-ONE

Nothing seemed any clearer an hour later as I headed up Highway 1 toward the Hollister Ranch. I'd checked in with the office; there were no more calls. So, after some hesitation, and a sandwich from my favorite deli, I'd started out in this direction.

The ranch driveway appeared on my left; indecision washed over me. Should I or shouldn't I?

Go on, I urged myself. Just find out what kind of alibis Travis and Bronc can give each other.

I swung the pickup into the drive, feeling committed. As I rolled slowly between silvery-gray skeletons of leafless cottonwood trees and green pastures fenced with weathered grape stakes, I wondered why in the world I was doing this. Someone had planted narcissus along the drive and their nodding heads were sharp yellow, cream, and orange against the brilliant green new grass, their very cheerfulness mocking me.

Afternoon sunshine lit the barnyard as I pulled in, reflecting off the whitewashed barns and fences, silvering the shingles of the employee houses. Everything was neat and well tended— with the sort of quiet winter tidiness appropriate to February. I could see the now bare canes of what looked like climbing roses festooning the adobe-brick wall around the ranch house. I imagined it was a colorful sight in summer.

I sat there for a few minutes, not sure what I wanted to do. No one appeared; the barnyard seemed deserted. No Bronc. No Travis. I began to relax a little.

My eyes roved, noting the familiar elements. A big concrete water trough in front of the largest barn with a spigot steadily dripping into it, chickens scratching the ground in front of the smaller barn, a tractor parked in one of the open bays of the shop. A gray cat was hunting gophers on the front lawn of the adobe ranch house, and I could see two horses, a sorrel and a bay, grazing in the field off to my right. Business as usual.

Eventually I got out of the truck. Still no one. The place was quiet, in the way that nature is quiet. Not the hushed, mechanical hum of a silent building, but a stillness interspersed with gentle sounds. A soft breath of a breeze, the faint screech of a seagull in the distance, the cluck of the chickens, and occasionally, as the wind shifted, the muffled noise of the surf. After a moment, I was aware of something else—a rhythmic pounding, punctuated by louder thuds, from the bullpen on the far side of the yard. I walked in that direction.

The bullpen had eight-foot-high solid walls. I could hear that someone, or something, was inside, but I couldn't see who or what. Built for breaking colts, the pen was about thirty feet in diameter. The gate had a small square hole cut in it, so that one could reach out, from inside, and open or close the latch. It was this hole that I approached.

Peering through, I could see Travis, with his back to me. He was working a roan colt from the ground; Trav stood in the center of the pen with a long bullwhip in his hand, and the colt loped around him, one eye constantly fixed on the man. The noise I'd heard was the sound of the colt's galloping hoofs, with louder raps when he'd strike the boards of the pen.

Automatically, my eyes went to the horse, observing and evaluating him. Red roan with a blaze face, he looked to be at least three years old, big and stout, a horse of the same type, and possibly the same breeding, as Willy. He had a saddle on his back, and he was packing it calmly, but judging by the wary expression in his eyes and the way Travis was working him, he probably hadn't been ridden much.

Travis, for his part, looked calm and serene, his face, when he turned to follow the motion of the horse around the pen, more relaxed than I'd seen it since Jack's murder. He seemed wholly absorbed in the colt; occasionally he clucked to him when he slowed, but otherwise he simply stood and watched the horse travel, never moving the whip at all.

I began to think that I might pass unnoticed, but the colt gave me away. Scent, or something, alerted him to my presence, and he snorted and shied as he went by the gate, his ears pointed sharply in my direction.

Travis looked to see what had alarmed him, and our eyes met. In an instant, the serenity on Trav's face vanished, to be replaced by the closest approach to fury I could imagine on that young and normally friendly countenance.

For a long moment we stared at each other and I began to revise my opinion on whether Travis would actually murder me in broad daylight in the Hollister Ranch yard. Glancing at my truck, I curbed the desire to bolt over to it and lock myself inside.

He wouldn't, I told myself. Bronc must be around here somewhere.

"What do you want?" Travis was striding toward the gate. The roan colt coasted to a stop at the far side of the corral and watched us, his eyes big.

Despite myself I began to back away. Travis jerked the latch open and stepped out of the bullpen, still carrying the bullwhip. I checked him over carefully, but I couldn't see that he had any other potential weapon. His jeans and T-shirt had no place to conceal a gun.

He's not going to kill you with that whip, I told myself, but my hands clenched themselves into defensive fists and I kept edging toward the truck.

"What are you doing here?" Trav demanded again as he strode toward me.

"Where's Bronc?" I asked, too nervous to answer his question, thinking only of safeguards against murder.

"Out doctoring cattle." Travis spoke curtly; he was standing right in front of me now, his coffee brown eyes, so like Jack's, hard and angry. Despite the fact that I'm a tall woman, I had to look up at him, and I felt suddenly aware of how much physically stronger he probably was.

Forcing myself not to cower, I looked straight into his eyes as he demanded once again, "What the hell are you doing here?"

"I came to see Bronc," I responded untruthfully.

"Leave the old man alone, why don't you? Isn't it bad enough that Jack's dead?"

"Bronc doesn't seem to mind me," I said firmly. "It's just you who's so upset."

"I know what you're doing." Travis shot back. "You're poking around making trouble because you don't want your friend to be arrested for murder. And you're not gonna pin it on me and Bronc. Or Laney," he added after a second.

"Is that why you're so upset?" I asked him. "Because I saw you at Laney's?"

"No." But for a moment he sounded a good deal less belligerent. "There's no law that says I can't date her. I didn't even know she used to be married to Jack when I asked her out," he added unnecessarily.

I waited, hoping he'd say more.

He didn't, though. He just stared back at me, his eyes still hot and hostile, but more controlled-looking. I was aware of the ranch surrounding us—the old barns and corrals like a silent audience. Travis had latched the gate to the bullpen, but I could hear the roan colt snort softly on the other side, as if he were listening, too.

"Did you know Jack was going to sell this ranch?" I asked.

No change in Trav's expression, just the same steady hostility he'd shown from the beginning. "Bullshit," he said.

"He was," I said mildly. "It's in escrow right now."

"That's bullshit. Jack left this ranch to the state, so that they could keep it the way it is."

"You want that, don't you?"

"Of course I do." Travis stared at me. "Why don't you just lay off?" he demanded. "You're not going to pin this murder on me or Bronc. We've got alibis. So does Laney. Pin it on Tara, if you want to pin it on somebody."

"I'd like to."

For a second Trav looked surprised, but the anger was back as quickly as it went away. "So go bother her, then, and leave us alone."

"Just what kind of alibi can you and Bronc give each other?"

As soon as the words were out of my mouth I knew I was in trouble. Trav's eyes blazed up into fury and I saw his fist tighten around the bullwhip. "None of your damn business," he said as he raised the whip.

I have no idea if he would really have hit me; I grabbed the whip as it came up. "Goddammit, Travis, knock it off. If you hit me with that thing, I'm going straight to the cops, and I know you don't want that."

It stopped him. For a moment, we stood like a piece of sculpture, eyes locked, both gripping the bullwhip; then I felt the tension drain out of his arm and I stepped back.

"Get out of here," he said.

Keeping a wary eye on him, I walked to the truck and climbed in. He made no move to harass or follow me, just stood there in the barnyard, watching me as I turned the pickup around and drove out. Animosity was plain in every line of his rigidly still form.

I knew as I drove away that I'd made an enemy for life. Travis wasn't going to forgive me. Maybe Jeri Ward was right. Maybe I was in over my head.

TWENTY-TWO

Ten minutes later, I was halfway back to the office, as depressed as I could remember being. Talk about useless and inept. I'd learned nothing and alienated Travis completely. Why, why couldn't I come up with something helpful—the hit man who'd assisted Tara, maybe, or someone else with a reason to murder Jack?

Someone else. The words rang a bell. Redwoods Inc. Who the hell was Redwoods Inc.? The developer, Denise had said. I had wondered if someone stood to gain or lose on Jack's upcoming deal, and I now knew the name of "someone." Sort of.

Picking up the car phone, I asked for the number of Redwoods Inc. The operator plugged me right into the recording—sounded like a Santa Cruz number. Without thinking about what I was going to say, I dialed it.

"Redwoods Incorporated." The receptionist had the faintest of southern drawls.

"Uh, this is the IRS," I ad-libbed desperately. "We're doing a routine check of our files and we need to update your address."

"It's 355 River Street, suite L," the secretary said, clearly puzzled. "The same as it was last year."

"Thanks very much," I said quickly and hung up. Well, that

was easy. And convenient. A right turn at the next stoplight and I was on River Street.

It took me a while to find 355, though, because River Street was a congested mass of urban development with a much less developed traffic system. Several huge warehouse-type discount stores, an indoor shopping mall, and innumerable strip malls created a consumer draw that the city streets were unable to deal with effectively. As a result, traffic always moved at a uniform crawl in this area.

Not being a big fan of retail therapy, I tended to avoid River Street like the plague, so not only did I not know exactly where I was going, I was unprepared for the abrupt lane changes, merges, and general maneuvering necessary to get from here to there. It took me a couple of passes through the worst of things to figure out which little strip mall bore the number 355, and by this time I was not in a good mood.

Barely restraining myself from flipping off an old lady who cut sharply in front of me with her Mercedes, I pulled into the parking lot of Redwood Village Shopping Center, with a muttered "Up yours." Silent cussing was allowed, but Jim would never forgive me for giving assholes the finger from the company truck.

I parked and got out, looking for suite L. Easier said than done. I discovered letters were alphabetically stenciled above each little business, but L was nowhere. There was K and then there was M. Where L should have been was just blank wall. I paced all the way up and down the place twice before I thought to go in and ask the clerk at a yogurt shop where L was.

"In back," she said. "That's the office."

Okay. I walked to the end of the mall for the third time and headed around behind it. Abruptly the superficially attractive veneer of neat sidewalks and brightly colored awnings gave way to a strictly utilitarian asphalted alley, with a high cinder-block wall on one side and the huge, undecorated, unwindowed mass of the building on the other. The alley was punctuated by a series of Dumpsters, from which trash spilled out in generous quantities. A fitful breeze tossed the empty coffee cups and other bits of detritus up and down the gutters, and the thin visible strip of winter sky above me seemed dimmed and chilly.

I kept walking, but my spirits, already low, plummeted right into my boots. I hated this. All the asphalt and concrete, the buildings and spaces without any beauty or character, the absence of any living things, and the sense that there was no place for them—I hated this world. One of the best points of my job was that it seldom took me to such places, and I was struck anew by the depressing thought that to many people this was the stuff of everyday life.

I could see a door ahead of me now, about halfway down the drafty alley, and I hurried. The bright winter day, so full of promise out at the Hollister Ranch, was a cold, dank affair in this bleak corridor.

The door—plain, metal, unwelcoming—had L stenciled above it. I pulled it open.

The hallway beyond almost made me turn back. A straight hard bowling alley leading off into the depths of the building, it had blank white walls and a concrete floor, illuminated by glaring fluorescent lights. As a place to get shot in a bad spy movie, it was perfect.

Timidly I started down it, feeling nervous as the exterior door closed behind me. God, now I was in the heart of the beast. Gobbled up by the modern world, never to see the sun again.

Shut up, Gail, I urged myself. This is a shopping center for God's sake, not a vision of hell. You couldn't tell it by me, though.

I passed a metal door marked Restrooms, and one that was locked, and finally came to one with a sign that said Offices. It opened when I tried it.

Inside was, sure enough, an office—desks, potted plants, copiers, computers, the usual. Two secretaries were visible, and the nearest one lifted her head at the sound of the door.

"Can I help you?"

By the voice, it was the receptionist who had answered the phone. Now what?

"I'm representing Travis Gunhart and Bronc Pickett of the Hollister Ranch" was what popped out of my mouth.

The secretary's eyes narrowed. "You'll be wanting Mr. Hoskins, then."

"Yes, that's right. Gail McCarthy," I added helpfully.

She got to her feet and stalked off across the office, walking with the stiff-legged gait of a woman in heels, and disappeared through an open door at the other end of the room. I could hear the murmur of voices, male and female, but I couldn't make out any words.

A minute or two passed, then the secretary reemerged. Behind her was a man. For a moment I was aware only that he looked familiar, and then recognition dawned. The beaked nose, the bald dome. Jesus Christ. I'd seen this man in the coffee shop of the Foresta Hotel in Tahoe. The man Jack had called Art.

Judging by the look in his eyes, he'd recognized me, too, and I didn't think he was happy about it. I had a strong desire to turn and run for the second time in one day, but I forced myself to stand my ground. Art, whoever he was, was not going to shoot me in front of two secretaries.

"Ms. McCarthy?" He was holding out his hand, but his expression was neutral, to say the least.

"Mr. Hoskins. I believe we've met. Up in Tahoe."

Art Hoskins's gaze flicked briefly to his secretary and then back to me. "Why don't you come into my office."

I followed him. It didn't look like a rich developer's office to me. Some dark mahogany furniture and maroon upholstery dignified it from the uniform beiges of the outer office, but it was still an unwindowed cell of a room, crowded with computer, printer, filing cabinets, a couple of potted plants, a large desk, and two swivel-type chairs. I sat down without being asked.

Art sat behind his desk and we studied each other. Whatever discomfort or alarm he'd felt at seeing me in his office was completely hidden now behind the quiet poker face of an experienced businessman. I tried to keep my own features equally still.

"So, Ms. McCarthy, what can I do for you?"

"Dr. McCarthy. We met up in Tahoe. In the coffee shop of the Foresta Hotel. I was with Jack Hollister. The night before he was killed." I watched the man carefully.

Art Hoskins shook his head. "That was a terrible thing." He waited.

I plunged on. "It turns out you and Jack were in the middle of making a deal on the Hollister Ranch."

"That's right."

"I hear you were in escrow when he was killed. How's that going to affect your deal?"

Art Hoskins said nothing.

I let the silence lie. It seemed to take a full minute, but eventually he spoke. "What do you have to do with this, Dr. McCarthy?"

"My friend's a suspect." Damned if I owed him any further explanations.

More silence. Art Hoskins looked composed, unruffled. For some reason, this was pissing me off. "Do the cops know you were up in Tahoe that night?" I asked him.

That got his attention. He didn't say a word, but his facial muscles tightened everywhere. No, I thought, they don't know, and he doesn't want them to.

The balance in the room had changed. Art still watched me closely; no obvious difference was apparent but I sensed the power lay with me.

"So what were you doing in Tahoe, Mr. Hoskins?"

Predictably, it took him a while to answer this question, and when he did his words were completely unexpected. "I used to be a horse vet."

"You're kidding."

He smiled, and for a second looked almost human. "It's been

years since I've practiced. But that's what I used to do. Up in the Bay Area. That's how I first met Jack."

"So why were you at the convention?"

"I'd been to it before. And I knew Jack would be there. We still had some loose ends to work out on the deal."

"So you were up there to see Jack."

"More or less. Ski. Take in a few lectures, maybe."

"Don't tell me. When you heard Jack had been murdered you beat feet for home."

Once again, Art was silent. I was trying to decide what to say, when he finally spoke. "I'd rather not be interviewed by the cops."

I was definitely one up.

"I had nothing to do with Jack's murder," he went on. "I've got a alibi for most of the evening; I was out with a group of old friends."

"But you spent the night alone?"

"Well, no."

"Then you have an alibi for the night."

"Not exactly." Unbelievably, I could see a faint flush on his cheekbones.

"A call girl?" I guessed.

He was quiet just a heartbeat too long. I studied his face. "A call boy?"

Almost imperceptibly, he nodded.

"So that's why you don't want to talk to the cops."

No response from Art, who looked clearly miserable.

"Could you produce the, uh, boy if you had to?"

"I don't know."

"I see," I said again. "If you'll answer my questions honestly, I'll keep my mouth shut about you unless I'm asked." My God. Jeri Ward would throw me in jail for this little bit of chicanery.

"So what do you want to know?" He sounded resigned.

"About this deal. If I have it right, Jack was planning to sell the Hollister Ranch to your company."

177

"That's right."

"So what were you going to do with the land?"

"Build a convention center. Condos. Some single-family housing."

For a brief second I had a vision of it, the old ranch that I'd seen not an hour ago reduced to a version of this modern hell— wall-to-wall asphalt and concrete, big cinder-block buildings, lots of multistoried gray condos. Yuck. The feeling was so strong I almost said the word out loud.

Instead I asked him, "You know that in Jack's will the ranch is to be left to the state, to be part of the state park."

"So I understand."

"So you're not going to end up with it now."

"That's debatable. We were in escrow. There were no obvious problems. Most of the paperwork is done. We're pursuing it."

We stared at each other. I understood that to Art the whole issue was nuts and bolts, dollars and cents. Any pleas to leave the old ranch be would be dismissed as ridiculous. A man who spent his days in a place like this, when he could obviously afford to be elsewhere, was not a man who would care that the Hollister Ranch was beautiful, and more than that, clothed with tradition.

Another question occurred to me. "Who gets the money, now, if the deal goes through?"

"Jack's estate, I assume."

Tara, Laney, and Karen. Shit. "How much is it, the purchase price, I mean?"

"Five and a half million."

"Oh." Good Lord. I couldn't even imagine having a million dollars in my possession, and Tara, lovely Tara, was going to end up with a good deal more than that.

There didn't seem to be much else to say. As I stood up to go, I asked him, "Just what is Redwoods Inc.?"

"A development company. We invest in properties we think we can make money on."

"It's your company?"

"I'm the president, and I own the majority of the shares. It's a corporation."

"Who are the other shareholders?" Maybe, I thought, just maybe, one of them would be someone I knew.

"Just some businessmen."

"Who?" I demanded.

Art Hoskins looked reluctant, but he knew I had him. "Carl Walters is one. Don Capelli. Henry Williams." Not names I recognized—not horse people.

"Anyone else?"

He sighed. "Jim Leonard."

"Not the Jim Leonard I work for?" I must have sounded as startled as I felt. He nodded resignedly.

"Did you know Jim was my boss?"

"Jack mentioned it, after I saw you in the coffee shop. I've known both Jim and Jack for years. Since I was in practice."

"Did you know they didn't get along?"

"It wasn't a problem." Art Hoskins said it easily but I wondered.

"Does Jim know this company he's involved in is trying to buy the Hollister Ranch?"

Art stared at me a minute. "It was Jim's idea," he said at last.

Good Lord. Jim's idea to buy the Hollister Ranch and make money on it. Some sort of bizarre revenge on Jack? It didn't make sense. Jack was willing to sell—apparently. Or had Jack changed his mind up there in Tahoe, maybe because he found out Jim was involved? Had Art Hoskins and Jim decided to kill Jack so that the deal would go through?

I didn't know what to think, or say. Jim couldn't be involved. Could he? Suddenly I didn't really want to know any more.

Art Hoskins was watching me, his emotionless expression calculated, his eyes steady. Once again the balance of power had shifted. This man doesn't really have an alibi, I told myself. And he might have a reason to have killed Jack.

Without a word, I turned and walked out of the room, making my way through the office and down the bleak hall. Walking around the mammoth building, I got in my truck, maneuvered my way out of the parking lot, through the congested mess on River Street, and onto the highway, all without seeing a thing.

The whole way back to the clinic I chased the same question, persistent as a dog in pursuit of its tail, but by the time I got there I wasn't any closer to the answer. Could Jim be involved in this murder? And if so, what should I do?

TWENTY-THREE

J im wasn't in evidence when I walked into our office, which was a relief. I didn't think I could have met his eyes. I checked the schedule and headed back out the door as fast as I could.

A couple of calls kept me busy for the rest of the afternoon. Fortunately they were easy ones—another mild colic case and a sole abscess. I couldn't have coped with anything too complicated. My brain was in a lather. What should I do? The words went round and round, as repetitive as the lyrics of a sappy song that sticks unrelentingly.

It was almost dark as I pulled in my driveway. Lifting Blue out of the truck, I trudged toward the front porch, fumbling through my pockets for the door key, paying no attention to my surroundings. I was face to face with the door when I noticed the square of white paper stuck to the wood with a tack. A note. Someone had left me a note.

It was folded. I pulled the tack out and opened the slip of paper. I almost dropped it.

Printed in hard, slanting capitals were the words BACK OFF OR DIE, BITCH. That was it. I stared stupidly, looking for a signature, a clue of some sort to who had done this. There was nothing. Of course there wasn't.

Hatred seemed to leap off the paper and take hold of my throat. The letters were deeply scored, violent.

Shaken, I clutched the note as I tried to get the key in the lock. I wanted inside, I wanted the door bolted, I wanted help.

I got the door open. Blue whined demandingly at me; he was already halfway down the steps to the yard. I peered at the deep shadows under the redwoods by the creek. No way did I want to go down there.

"You go," I told the old dog.

Obediently he stumped down the steps. I stood close to the door, waiting, watching him, trying to watch the street and everything else around me at the same time. Whoever had left the note might be hiding, watching, stalking me.

Shit. This was not a good thought. "Come on, Blue," I urged him. "Hurry up."

It seemed to take forever, but eventually he made his slow way back up the steps. To my relief, the cat was with him; I'd had a brief, sick image of Bonner's body hanging upside down somewhere, some sort of sadistic warning. Thank God he was all right.

I let the animals in the house, locked and bolted the door, and sat down next to the phone with the note in my hand. I looked around. Everything looked normal. No sign that anyone had been inside.

Okay. Call the police. Ask for Jeri Ward.

But I didn't. "Back off or die, bitch."

I stared at the note. Travis? Tara? I tried to decide if the printing looked male or female.

Art Hoskins? But how would he know where I lived? He could have called Jim, I thought. Jim knew where I lived.

Another thought intruded. Joanna knew my address. But Joanna was in Merced, or had been when I called her last night. She wouldn't drive two and a half hours to leave a note on my door. Would she?

I got up and pulled all the window curtains shut. What should I do? The same old refrain.

My little house was tainted. Someone had been here intending to harm me. Someone had invaded my space. Suddenly I was more angry than scared. All right, you sons-of-bitches, you'll see. Back off? Not a chance.

I went downstairs and got the pistol out of its locked cupboard. Checking to be sure there was no bullet in the chamber, I brought it up and set it on the kitchen table. I looked in the refrigerator. Then I went back to the phone.

I didn't call Jeri Ward. I called Lonny.

He answered on the second ring, sounding as cheerful as usual. Just the thought of him made me smile.

"So," I said, "how would you like to come over for dinner?"

"Should I pack my toothbrush?"

"Yes."

TWENTY-FOUR

I made clam chowder for dinner. Mostly out of cans, I will admit, but I added some bacon and celery I had in the fridge, thickened it up with butter and two or three potatoes that were languishing in the cupboard, and embellished the whole thing heavily with black pepper. A bottle of local chardonnay and the tail end of a loaf of French bread concealed any deficiencies. Lonny looked content and Blue and Bonner finished the remnants happily.

After some deliberation, I'd decided not to mention the note to Lonny. I didn't want him turning overly protective on me. His presence alone, I reckoned, would make me safe enough. Putting the note in a drawer, I'd locked the gun back in its cupboard and greeted Lonny with a cheerful smile.

Dinner and a couple of glasses of wine behind me, I found the note didn't prey on my mind much, anyway. Not with Lonny sitting on the couch next to me, his shoulder touching mine as he skimmed the evening paper.

Not when he put his arm around me and kissed me, either, or when he began unbuttoning my shirt. I merely cast a quick glance around the room to make sure the curtains were still shut and the dead bolt was shot home, and then stretched my hand out and took hold of his belt buckle.

"Here?" he said in my ear.

"Why not?"

For the next hour I lost myself in sex, in the kissing and pressing, the arousal and entering, the long, slow build to the mind-emptying climax. And then, lying together on the couch, half asleep and wholly relaxed, I let myself drift into peaceful forgetfulness. Until the first shot rang out.

A blasting, electrifying crack, it stood me bolt upright in a half second. Lonny was slower to react, not being primed for trouble.

"What the hell was that?" He stared up at me from the couch.

"A shot. Oh shit."

Another crack and then two more in rapid succession.

I dove onto the floor. Blue pressed himself against me, whining; he'd always hated gunshots.

"Jesus Christ," Lonny roared, scrambling off the couch and searching frantically for his clothes.

Two more earsplitting explosions. Where the hell were the bullets going?

I could feel Blue trembling next to me, and the cat scooted across the room and hid under the couch. I pressed my naked body to the rug.

Another violent bang. Blue whimpered. I could see Lonny struggling to pull his pants on, bare feet clumping in front of my nose.

A rippling series of bangs went off, raising the hair on the back of my neck. God damn them.

Leaping to my feet, I ran toward the door. I grabbed the heavy black flashlight I kept on the dresser. Those bangs had come from the other side of the creek.

"Wait, Gail; don't!"

I could hear Lonny shouting, but I was too angry to care. I shoved the bolt back and opened the door. Sheltering behind

185

it, I pointed the flashlight beam toward the creek.

"Knock it off, asshole!" I screamed at the top of my voice, scanning the tangled brush on the far bank. "Call 911!" I hurled at Lonny.

Playing the flashlight over the creek bank, I searched for movement, for shapes that shouldn't be there. Nothing. Only tangled willows and cottonwoods, spikes of Monterey pine and redwood. I swung the light toward my driveway. Nothing out of place there, either. Lonny's Bronco and my pickup sat quietly side by side.

But there was a dirt road on the other side of the creek, I knew. Someone was over there in the brush hiding.

I held my breath. Only silence met me. The noise had stopped the moment I opened the door. No shots. I couldn't hear any crashing in the brush, either.

Swinging the flashlight beam across my driveway, I saw a flash of white in the gravel, like a cigarette stub. Only I never, ever left any litter in my driveway. Not to mention I didn't smoke. Nor did Lonny.

I stepped out the door and, picking my way gingerly over the gravel on bare feet, bent toward the odd white tube. It had a slender wire attached to one end, and, on close inspection was actually a sort of blue and white striped pattern. There was a faint smell of sulfur when I sniffed it.

Bottle rocket. I remembered them from my rowdy high school years. Illegal, but easily acquirable. Kids bought them in Chinatown, in Mexico. They made a hell of a bang.

They hadn't been shots at all. Bottle rockets going off overhead, that was all.

But why? I straightened up and, for the first time, saw the exterior side of the door I'd been hiding behind. There was a note on it. Caught between fright and fury, I went to get it, and found myself grabbed roughly by the arm and jerked into the house.

"Goddammit, Gail, get inside." Lonny was wearing only his jeans.

"They were bottle rockets," I said, clutching the note.

Lonny slammed the door. "I figured that out for myself. The noise was wrong for shots. But you're still an idiot for running out there naked."

I stared down at my body. I was, indeed, naked. Well, of course I was naked. I'd started out naked and I'd never put any clothes on.

"I suppose I did look a little silly."

"You looked ridiculous." Lonny was still irate. "Not to mention you were a sitting duck if those had been shots. What got into you?"

"I don't know. First I was scared and then I didn't care what happened to me; I wanted to attack whoever was shooting at us." I shivered. "Adrenaline, I guess. It was stupid."

Lonny abandoned his anger suddenly and pulled me close. "You dummy," he said affectionately. "You're freezing."

"Did you call 911?"

"No, not yet. I knew they weren't shots, just firecrackers. Probably kids, fooling around. But why here?"

I unfolded my fingers from around the note. "Because of this, I guess."

"What's this?"

I held the note so we could both read it. NEXT TIME IT WILL BE FOR REAL. YOU'VE BEEN WARNED.

The same hard slanting capitals. I went over to the dresser and got the first note and showed it to Lonny. "I found this one on the door when I got home."

"What the hell?" Lonny was staring at the two notes, his expression confused. "Gail, what've you been doing?"

"Poking around."

"You'd better quit doing it. And take these notes to the police. This is about Jack's murder, isn't it?"

I reached down and picked up the faded quilt that lay over one arm of the couch and wrapped it around myself. "Yes." I held up a hand to stop him as he opened his mouth. "Don't press me. I need some time to think. There's something funny about all this."

Lonny looked reluctant. "It's your decision, I guess. But I think you ought to go to the police."

I stood on tiptoe and kissed his mouth. "I need one more favor."

"What's that?"

"Loan me your truck and trailer tomorrow."

"Why?"

"Because I need to borrow them."

Lonny stared at me, worry lines creasing the skin around his eyes. "All right," he said slowly, "if that's what you need. But be careful."

"I will," I said. I meant it, too.

TWENTY-FIVE

At ten the next morning I unloaded Gunner in a sandy, windswept parking lot just north of Santa Cruz. I told the receptionist I was taking the day off without giving a reason. Let Jim wonder.

So here I was, saddling my horse on a shiny winter morning, all set to go for a ride on the beach. My heart should have been singing, but it wasn't.

I finished saddling and bridling Gunner, locked the truck and the tack box of the trailer, shoved the keys in my pocket, and climbed aboard. Ignoring the colt's wide eyes and reluctant steps, I urged him toward a trail through the sand dunes that I'd taken several times before. Of course, I'd always been with Lonny and we'd always been on Burt and Pistol. This was Gunner's first trip to the beach and our first solitary expedition together.

We threaded our way between the dunes, the wind bending the sedge grass around us, the sound of the surf growing steadily louder. Down a little gully, Gunner's feet sinking and slipping in the loose sand, and there it was. Immense, endless, loudly overpowering—the sea.

Clear winter air gave the beach a crystalline sharpness—so

intense I had to shut my eyes for a second. White sand, blue sky, each wave that impossibly lovely translucent blue-green, crashing in a dazzle of foam to the shore. Restless and lively, the water glittered, its overwhelming presence filling the horizon, cascading in a constant roar on the stretch of sand before me.

A chilly breeze whipped my hair off my ears and lifted Gunner's mane. I sat transfixed, staring at the blindingly bright noisy ocean as if I'd never seen it before. Gunner stared, too, his ears up, his eyes big. As far as I knew, he had, in fact, never seen it before. He didn't seem scared, though. More fascinated and excited.

It was a different story when I urged him forward. Snorting, he raised his head and stiffened his body; I could read the message perfectly. Not on your life, he was telling me; that's all right to look at, but I'm not going near it.

Much persistent thumping on his sides, mixed with a couple of sharp taps from the spurs and some firm guidance from the reins, eventually convinced him that he had to, and with many sudden swerves breaking our progress, we advanced to the edge of the surf. I kept one hand tightly wrapped around the saddle horn; Gunner, bred to be a cutting horse, could leap sideways so abruptly that I might have fallen off otherwise.

I contemplated making him enter the water, but gave it up as a bad idea; even Burt, my mount on previous rides, hated to do that, though he would go, if forced. Lonny had told me the secret—"The way you get a horse in the surf is to back him in." He'd accustomed Burt and Pistol like this, and I supposed I could do it with Gunner, but I didn't feel up for a struggle, at the moment.

Instead, I rode along the beach, Gunner's feet sinking slightly in the wet sand beside the water. A fine mist of salt spray blew in our faces as the surf pounded and crashed beside us, noisy and violent, full of sudden clashes of light. My left arm grew tired from constantly correcting his drift away from the breakers, and the fingers of my right hand were sore from my death grip on the horn, but apart from occasional leaps at encroaching waves, he behaved quite well.

Some twenty minutes down the beach I saw the oak tree I'd been looking for, and crossed the deeper sand to take a trail that wound through the dunes and then up into the hills. It was a trail I'd taken before; it followed the hilly country along the shore for a while and eventually emerged into a meadow that offered a fairly spectacular view of the north coast. With the Hollister Ranch in the foreground.

Gunner was plugging along now; his eyes and ears were still working, but the light sweat on his neck had taken the edge off his spookiness. I stopped to open an old wooden gate, and he stood quietly, tired enough to behave. In another ten minutes we reached the place I'd been aiming for—a rough, coastal meadow with a view to end all views. Halting Gunner, I faced the ocean.

The wind blew in my face, making a sharp silvery whine in my earrings. The Pacific had a cold edge today; the sea was rough and restless, whitecaps everywhere. From the scrubby hillside where I stood I could see the Hollister Ranch headquarters, huddled in the hollow below me, and beyond that, demanding my attention, lay the dramatic, rocky coastline to the north.

Everything was brilliant and hard, the dark, jagged promontories sharply etched against the clear winter sky and the turbulent sea. Gunner snorted at a sudden flare of rustles as the wind beat at a nearby bunch of pampas grass; everywhere greasewood and patches of thin grass moved and jerked in the air currents.

This north coast country, I thought, though beautiful, was bleak and inhospitable, a place to visit, not a place to live. It was either foggy or windy ninety percent of the time, and I found the ocean, though spectacular, an oppressive, almost ominous presence after a while—too big, too impersonal, just too damn cold.

I looked back at the Hollister Ranch, trying to see it with the eyes of love. The old, carefully tended barns and well-repaired fences, the cottonwoods lining the drive and the stream running through the pasture, the walled garden behind the adobe ranch house, with its neat orchard and ancient climbing roses festooning the whitewashed bricks. Cattle grazed in a small field just below me, bordered by the beach, the red and black shapes of the cows and calves impossibly picturesque against a background of new green grass and rolling winter surf.

A person could love this, I thought. A person could love the ocean, too; it was possible. Many people did. It was no doubt some fault in my own nature that rendered it forbidding.

I don't know how long I stood there, staring and thinking. Long enough that I started to get cold. I was in the process of running the zipper on my sweatshirt up to the top and tying my hood firmly over my head when Gunner pricked his ears. His gaze was focused back down the trail, in the direction from which we'd come. His body stiffened.

In a second I saw what his more acute senses had foreseen— a horse and rider coming up the trail. Bronc, I realized a moment later. Bronc and the newly dark brown, bobtailed Willy.

For a second, indecision rushed over me. I'd come out here for a solitary ride, to think, not to talk to Bronc. But here he was. He'd seen me, certainly. I could hardly dive Gunner into the scrub and gallop off at this point. So I held still, patting Gunner's neck to reassure him, awaiting Bronc's approach.

He rode up to me quietly, nodding in greeting. He'd been out checking cattle presumably; Willy was carrying saddlebags and there were two ropes tied to the saddle.

"Hi, Bronc," I said.

"Well hello, sweetheart." He didn't look at me as he said it; he was scanning the pasture, his eyes sharp under the brim of his cowboy hat.

"You out doctoring?" I asked him.

"Yes, ma'am. A couple of those young calves had the scours

this morning. I found one and gave him a shot of penicillin, but I can't locate the other."

For a second we were quiet, both of us looking over the Hollister Ranch, before he fixed his hard, old eyes on my face. "You ever figure out who killed Jack?"

"I'm working on it."

"So what've you come up with?"

"You said you could give Travis an alibi," I began, and he glanced at me sharply. "I don't think that's true," I went on.

"The kid had nothing to do with it." Bronc's voice was harsh, an old man's voice. "You don't know one thing about it if you think Travis had anything to do with killing Jack."

For a long moment Bronc stared steadily at the ranch below us. "Travis hasn't got anything in the world but that ranch," he said slowly. "When he came here he was just sixteen, and he'd run away from some big city back east—Chicago, he said. I guess his mom was dead and his dad knocked him around a lot. So he just run away. Came out west to be a cowboy." Bronc chuckled.

"People used to say he was really Jack's illegitimate kid."

"People say a lot of things. Jack was sterile like I told you. When he was married to the first one there was a lot of carrying on about it. I knew."

Bronc leaned off the side of Willy and spat reflectively. "Travis never did want anything to do with his family; maybe that's what got the talk going. People figured Jack must be his real dad, 'cause the kid didn't have anyone else.

"But I remember like it was yesterday the morning that boy came walking down the drive. He was wearing a clean shirt and jeans and carrying a little bag no bigger than one of these saddlebags. Everything he owned was in that bag. I was cutting up a big old dead oak in the front pasture and he walked right up to me and asked for a job."

I could see it in my mind, such was Bronc's storytelling; the kid, poor but clean, the old man out in the pasture, working.

"Now I wouldn't've hired any old bum who walked down my driveway, but this looked like a good kid and I thought I could use some help that day. So I said, 'I'll give you a day's work.' " Bronc shook his head. "And damned if he hasn't been here ever since."

"Did you hire him to stay on or did Jack?" I asked curiously.

"I did. Jack left all that sort of thing to me." Bronc's chin lifted. "Trav's all right, sweetheart. I know that boy; he may have a temper, but he hasn't got any meanness in him. Travis could no more have shot Jack than he could've jumped over the moon."

"Did you know he was seeing Laney? Jack's ex."

Bronc laughed, a short, sharp bark. "Is that right? Well, I wouldn't mind seeing her myself."

"It gives him a motive, though. Laney's inheriting a lot of money." I waited, watching for Bronc's reaction.

He just looked steadily at me. "What I'm telling you is that Travis wouldn't do anything to hurt Jack, or to hurt his own chances of staying here on this ranch. He hasn't got anywhere else to go."

"What if," I said slowly, "he knew Jack was about to sell the ranch to some developers?"

For a second Bronc's impassive eyes were startled, but the expression was gone as fast as it came. "Wouldn't make no difference. Travis wouldn't have killed Jack."

"I still don't think you can give him an alibi, Bronc," I said gently.

"Sweetheart, you are barking up the wrong tree." Bronc's voice was hard. "I'm telling you Travis didn't do it."

"I think Travis is lying," I said quietly, watching Bronc the whole time. "I think that's why he's been so upset. I think he was over at my house last night, trying to scare me into staying out of this."

"Travis had nothin' to do with killing Jack." Bronc wouldn't meet my eyes.

"Okay," I agreed equably. "Maybe he didn't. Maybe he's trying to protect you. He knows you weren't on the ranch, because he was. He's afraid you were up in Tahoe."

There was a long moment of silence. Bronc's eyes flicked at mine and then away again. Shit. Why had I said it? I'd been thinking of this since yesterday, but I hadn't meant to put it directly to Bronc. I'd only meant to go on a ride and look at the ranch, see if I could understand any better.

Bronc's face had the appearance of carved oak, lined and brown, the same wooden consistency. Nothing in his eyes that I could read.

"The way I figure it," I went on deliberately, "you killed Jack to keep the ranch from being developed into housing tracts." Put baldly like that, it sounded ridiculous.

Still staring at Bronc, I tried to imagine what was in his mind. Grief? Anger? He seemed beyond all that, sitting there on his horse with his cowboy hat pulled low on his forehead, his coiled ropes at his side. More an icon than a man, an image welded to a tradition, the symbol of a way of life.

Eventually he smiled, or what passed with him as a smile. I'd noticed before that though he laughed and joshed and flashed those teeth a lot, he never really smiled.

"Are you gonna turn me in?" He said it almost lightly.

I gazed back at him. Maybe I should have been frightened, but I wasn't. It seemed impossible to be afraid of Bronc; we'd spent too much time sitting on arena railings together, teasing each other. I couldn't believe he'd hurt me.

Not answering his question, I asked him another. "Why'd you do it, Bronc? I mean I know why, sort of, but how could you? Jack was your friend."

Bronc turned his face away from me and looked back down at the ranch. For a long moment I thought he wouldn't answer, then he cleared his throat roughly.

"You didn't know Jack Hollister," he said, not taking his eyes off the ranch. "Didn't anybody know Jack Hollister but me."

TWENTY-SIX

What do you mean?" I asked him.

"Jack wasn't like people thought he was." Bronc kept not looking at me as he spoke, directing his talk to the ranch and the ocean beyond. "Ever since I've known him, ever since he was a kid, he could fool people. He had this nice way about him and he liked to make people like him, but Jack didn't really care about anything.

"I found that out early, right after Len died and Jack inherited the place. First thing he did was sell all Len's horses. Shit. Len worked his whole life to develop that horse herd. He loved those horses. Second only to the way he loved the ranch. Well, I already knew Jack wouldn't listen to anything, so I never said a word, I just asked him if he'd let me keep a couple of 'em. And he said sure; one thing about Jack—he liked to give people things. It made him feel good."

Bronc patted Willy's neck briefly. "One of those mares I kept was his mother. But anyway, about Jack, I don't know if I can make you understand how he was. He never cared about the land or the livestock except to make money on 'em, and he never gave a damn about any human being that ever lived, except as how that person made him feel good. And he never had any heart. Not from day one.

"I remember that first summer I worked here, I was teachin' him to ride colts and he was the most athletic son-of-a-bitch I ever laid eyes on. It all came natural to him. He rode those crooked, wicked suckers like it was as easy as a stroll in the park. And then one of them—a little grulla gelding it was—got ahead of him and doubled back and dumped his ass on the ground. And that great big kid just got up and walked off. He comes back five minutes later with Len's gun, and damned if he didn't want to shoot that horse."

Bronc leaned over and spat. "I knew all about Jack from that first summer, knew what he was and how different he was from his old man. Len was a good man, and Jack was his only kid; I guess Jack's mama died in childbirth, that's what I heard, anyway. So Len gave that kid any damn thing he wanted. And it just plain ruined Jack."

"So it was all right to kill him?" These were my first words since Bronc had started talking and he rebutted them with a flash of anger.

"Honey, you don't understand. I spent a lifetime with that son-of-a-bitch, and I don't know how to tell you what I knew about him. Only interested in Jack and playin' the goddamn big rancher—never gave a shit about anyone or anything else. That will he made, leavin' the ranch to the state—it was just because I asked him to. He didn't care about the ranch, but he always wanted me to like him. All his life he wanted me to think he was a big man, like everyone else did, and he knew I didn't. He was always trying to impress me."

"Didn't that make you like him a little?"

"Hell, no. I felt sorry for him sometimes, but mostly I felt sorry for ever' living thing he came in contact with."

"So why'd you stay with him?"

"I didn't stay with him. I stayed on the ranch. Len, Jack's old man, he loved this ranch. He was raised on it, his daddy built it, and he told me more'n once how much it meant to his pa. I got to where I loved it, too. I wasn't goin' to leave it to Jack. Len didn't understand about Jack. Like most folks, I guess, he wanted to see the best in his kid. But I knew Jack would let the old place fall apart. He just didn't give a damn."

"But you went team roping with him. You hung around with him."

Bronc was silent awhile, looking down on the ranch, his hands folded quietly over the saddle horn. "Honey, it's hard to make you understand," he said at last, his voice rough. "It's like we were married to each other. One of those deals where you've been together forever and you more or less hate each other, but it's the only life you know."

Wind flurried in the pampas grass with a paperlike rustling, causing Gunner to cock a watchful ear. I thought about bad marriages and how they could be when people, for whatever reason, elected to stay and endure.

"I still don't understand how you could have killed him," I said finally.

"What the hell do you care? You didn't give a damn about Jack."

I was silent. In a sense, Bronc was right. I knew Jack as well, or as little, as I knew dozens, really hundreds of other people. He was just one of the many human beings who were part of the background of my life. Since his death, I'd been forced to recognize how slight that sort of knowing was. In fact, it was clear to me that I probably wouldn't have liked Jack if I had known him better. It had been shocking to think of him being killed, but no, I hadn't felt any grief over Jack.

I had felt a sense of dismay, though, and a strong sense of wrongness. *This shouldn't have happened* were the words that formed themselves in my mind.

"Murder is wrong," I said flatly. Simplistic, I know, but what else could I say? "To kill someone, other than to save your life, or protect someone else's, is wrong."

198

Bronc leaned off to one side of Willy and spat. "What about those bastards I killed in Korea?"

I shook my head. "That's different," I told him, and was aware of how lame it sounded.

He waved his hand at the view in front of us. The old ranch, weathered in its hollow, the sheer hard drama of the rough coastline. "Isn't this worth more than most of the damn human beings you know?"

I had no answer. I stared at the land, graceful and harsh, and knew that to him it held the depth and power of home. What was it worth? My own childhood home, an apple farm in the Soquel hills, had been developed into housing tracts. What would I have done to save it? Killed another human being in cold blood?

"You shouldn't have killed Jack," I said finally. "You can't go around killing people, no matter how noble your motive is. It's just plain wrong. I can understand why you did it, but it was still wrong."

Bronc snorted. "What's wrong is to tear up this piece of land and build condos over it. And there purely wasn't any other way to save it. I tried. I argued with that son-of-a-bitch until I was blue in the face when he first told me what he planned to do. He wouldn't hear a word I said. Then, not but two weeks ago, I asked him if he still planned to sell the ranch. It's a done deal, he told me, I'll be signing the papers next week when I get back.

"Over my dead body, I told him, and he said, Well you better hurry up and die then. Oh, he thought it was all a big joke. You'll like this place I'm buying in San Benito County, he told me.

"Well, I looked him right square in the eye and said, I can't let you do this, Jack, your daddy would turn in his grave if he knew you would do something like this. You can't stop progress, pardner, was all he said." Bronc spat again. "The hell I can't, I told him. I can stop you. And Jack, he just turned and walked off. He signed his own warrant as far as I was concerned."

"But how could you actually kill him?"

"Honey, I did him a favor. I've shot upwards of a dozen old horses in my life, when their time was up, and I know how to do it. I'd put a little grain on the ground, and when their head was down, eating, I'd shoot 'em right between the eyes. They never felt a thing. I just took that old twenty-two, that I kept for the horses, and I did Jack the same way. He never knew what hit him."

"You filed the serial numbers off the gun and you probably wore gloves, didn't you?"

"Yup, I bought that gun years ago, but I figured it was best to be safe."

"And the silencer? Did you make it?"

"I sure did. Made it myself, right in that shop down there, out of a piece of lead pipe."

"And you waited in that glass-fronted coffee shop until you spotted Jack gambling."

"Now that's pretty sharp of you." Bronc actually looked pleased. "I wore this big slicker I had and carried the gun in the pocket. I just sat in there and read the paper until I saw Jack in the casino, gambling with that blonde. All I had to do was wait till he went out on the deck."

"How'd you know he would be there, or that he'd go out on the deck?"

"Well, I didn't know exactly, but I knew Jack. I'd gone up to Tahoe with him before, when he went to this vet conference. He always stayed in the same hotel and he always gambled at that same casino. And every time, when we were there before, he went out on that deck to look at the lake and smoke. So I waited."

"And when he went out the back door, you went out after him and shot him." The words chilled me.

"He never felt a thing," Bronc said again, defensively. "I know where to shoot a man from my time in Korea. Right at the base of the neck. He never saw me coming and he never felt one thing. I just pitched him over the railing into the lake and pitched the gun after him and walked back into the bathroom. No one noticed anything."

I could picture him doing it all right. I felt a sudden spurt of anger. "It won't work, anyway. The ranch was in escrow. The developers will probably still end up with it. You killed him for nothing."

Bronc's eyes shot to my face and I saw instantly that I'd made a big mistake. He'd gambled everything and he wasn't prepared to lose.

"The hell I did," he said, and for the first time I was afraid.

I picked Gunner's reins up off his neck, with the vague but powerful sense that I needed to get out of here. Bronc wasn't looking at me, he was fiddling with his rope, and I kicked Gunner forward.

There was a whizzing sound and I flinched as something jerked my arms tight to my sides at the elbows. He'd roped me, I realized a split second later, flung the loop over my head and shoulders in the effortless, offhand style of a cowboy corral-roping horses.

I turned and looked back at him and for a moment that seemed to occur in slow motion, we stared into each other's eyes, my sense of shocked disbelief giving way to real fear. That hard, implacable quality I'd seen once before—this wasn't the Bronc I knew. I clutched the horn with one hand and stabbed Gunner hard with the right spur.

Snorting, he cleared twenty feet in one great sideways swoop; I hung on desperately and spurred him again. I could see Bronc struggling to dally as the rope ran through his surprised hands, and then Gunner bolted forward in earnest, headed for the trail back down the hill.

Clinging to the horn with one half-confined hand, my body tense with fear, I waited for the jerk from behind that would snatch me off the horse and slam me to the ground. It didn't come. I could feel the rope trailing free behind me; we'd managed to yank it out of Bronc's hands.

Gunner was galloping now, running downhill, and it took every atom of skill I had to stay balanced on top of him with my arms pulled to my sides. My grip of the saddle horn was all that was saving me, that and the fact that I hadn't lost my stir-rups. Still, the lurching, catapulting nature of his headlong, downhill gallop had my heart in my throat as I struggled frantically to stay on.

He slowed slightly when he reached a level spot, and I seized the chance to wriggle and twist my arms free of the now slack rope. In another second I flung the noose over my head and picked up the reins.

Gunner slowed still more when he felt me take control, and I looked back over my shoulder. Bronc was charging down the hill behind us, loop whirling—like any good ranch cowboy he carried a second rope.

Heart pounding, I dug my spurs into Gunner's ribs, sending him forward with a jump. Once again the landscape accelerated into a jerking rush—the brushy hillside barely perceived in my peripheral vision as I focused on the trail in front of me, striving to stay with Gunner's rhythm as he plunged down the grade. Every log, every hummock assumed a major importance as I tried to keep my weight balanced in the right spot.

Despite my fear, I didn't look back. I needed my eyes forward, straight between his ears, looking where we were going, just to stay on. I knew Bronc was back there, knew he could outride me, out-cowboy me, and probably rope me with ease. My only hope was to ride like hell.

Urging Gunner forward with my body, I tried to be part of him, running downhill as fast as I could go. I could feel the thud of his feet, hear his snorting breath, see his ears flicking forward and back to me. Through my fear, I felt a rushing exhilaration.

Then it hit me. The gate. I'd forgotten the gate.

I could see it up ahead, solid, wooden, blocking the way back to the truck. No way to open it, not with Bronc right behind me. Jump it?

Shit. We were getting closer, Gunner galloping hard. The old gate had sunk so that it was only about three feet at the low end; any horse can jump three feet. Can, but won't, maybe. As far as I knew, Gunner had never jumped anything.

I urged him on, drumming my heels in his sides, keeping my weight forward, aiming for the low spot. "Come on, boy."

It was only a few strides away and I could feel him begin to slow. I put everything—my body, my legs, my hands—into a smooth continuous urge. I sent myself forward. I could feel him surge, he gathered himself, I knew he would jump.

He hesitated a split second and then leapt. My neck snapped backward, I grabbed wildly at the horn in midair; it felt like he'd gone six feet straight up.

We cleared the gate and hit the ground on the other side with a solid, bone-jerking thud. Gunner was no lady's hunter. But we were over and okay. I kicked him forward and looked back.

Bronc and Willy were thundering toward us—to my dismay the old man's face was clearly determined. No gate would stop him if it hadn't stopped me.

Willy was hesitating, checking; Bronc kicked steadily, but I could see in the horse's eyes that he wouldn't do it. Bronc knew, too, and he whipped Willy over and under with the whirling rope. Crack, crack—the loop lashed Willy's flanks and he leaped forward, making a halfhearted attempt to jump.

The gate exploded. Boards shrieked and split. Willy hit it dead on with his chest and the old lumber shattered apart. For a moment, I thought the horse would go down, but he gathered himself and plowed through, shards of wood flying around him, Bronc still squarely in place.

Shit. My eyes went back to the trail ahead of me and I clucked to Gunner. We had to get away from Bronc.

The trail was merging into the dunes; Gunner plunged over a little rise and down into the loose sand, stumbling and almost falling. He caught himself as I fell forward over his withers, just barely hanging on by his mane, my heart lodging in the back of my mouth.

Stay up, buddy, stay up, I pleaded silently as he floundered and wallowed, trying to run through the deep sand. It was terribly difficult, I knew; I could feel the struggling force of his exertion.

Still, I urged him on. A quick glance showed Bronc right behind, his rope whirling, Willy plunging heavily. I had to get on the beach, where there might be some people around.

Gunner was driving forward in great, leaping bounds as he sank into the deep sand and pushed out, but the surf was in sight and I clucked to him and urged him toward the hard, wet sand. In a moment we were on it and headed toward the rig, though there was still no one in sight.

Willy was right on my heels. I could hear his thundering strides and almost feel the whistle of Bronc's loop. I clucked frantically to Gunner, squeezing and urging with hands and feet as his gallop smoothed out on the firmer ground. His ears flicked back and then he squirted forward in a renewed burst of effort, his stride lengthening smoothly.

I had no idea how fast he could run; I'd never galloped him flat out before. What I did know was that Willy was a very fast horse. Without looking back, I begged Gunner with my body—faster, faster.

He accelerated, the surf and sky and sand blurring around me, the cold, salty wind bringing tears to my eyes. I was aware only of his stretched-out neck and head in front of me, his driving rhythmic strides beneath me. The whole world—Bronc and the danger he represented—disappeared; I was lost in the race, determined to win.

I don't know how long we ran before I realized there were no longer any following hoofbeats. Eventually it sank in. Looking over my shoulder, I saw that Bronc and Willy were gone. With a gasp of triumph and relief, I pulled Gunner up and looked back.

Bronc was still visible, a cowboy-hatted figure on a dark horse, staring after me. After a minute he waved and wheeled Willy away. I could see him riding up the beach toward the ranch.

I took a deep, shuddering breath. Gunner had outrun Willy. We'd won.

TWENTY-SEVEN

For some long moments I stood there, staring after Bronc's solitary figure until he disappeared in the dunes. A flock of seagulls flew overhead, squawking and screeching in loud cacophony; the ocean rolled and crashed in front of me, blowing spray in my face, but I barely heard or saw any of it. I was listening to my heart beat, feeling the tension drain out of my body.

When I finally felt calm enough to ride on, I clucked to Gunner. He took a step and stumbled, and I realized in sudden alarm that he was shaking with exhaustion. His whole body was wet with sweat and white with foam, his heart moved my legs in great pounding thumps, and his flanks gasped in and out like bellows. I jumped off quickly and saw that his front legs were trembling.

A different sort of fear washed over me as I led him forward at the walk, and I prayed to God I hadn't hurt him. Walking him a few steps, I checked to see that he was still sound; then I let him stop and breathe. Then a few more steps and a rest. I felt each of his legs in turn; they were smooth and clean. But his flanks heaved as if he'd never get enough air, his red, flaring nostrils gasping and sucking. Patting his sweaty neck, I murmured over and over, "I'm sorry, I'm sorry."

What I had done was criminal, unforgivable, for any other reason than to save my life. With that threat removed, I was aghast at the colt's condition. Had I really needed to do this to him? Would Bronc actually have hurt me?

I didn't know, but I did know now that Bronc had killed Jack and I was presently a threat to him. And he probably could guess where I'd parked the rig, I thought a split second later.

There were still no people around; this north coast beach was as deserted as I'd ever seen it. I began to hurry a little, coaxing Gunner to walk as fast as he could.

Eventually we reached the trailer. There were a few cars in the parking lot, though I still didn't see any actual living human beings. Unlocking the truck and trailer, I unsaddled Gunner, and deciding to take a chance on Bronc's potentially imminent arrival, I began walking the colt in circles. Twenty minutes later I was still walking him, and Bronc hadn't arrived.

He wasn't planning on pursuing me. The ball was in my court. Just what I should do with it I didn't know. The obvious choice was to trot on down and tell Jeri Ward all about it, but I was determined to take care of Gunner first. So I walked him until the sweat was dry and he was cool, then blanketed him and put him in the trailer, and took him home.

Back at Lonny's I checked him over carefully once more; he truly seemed to be all right, just tired. I gave him and Plumber a flake of oat hay and leaned on the fence, watching them eat.

I ought to do something, I thought. I've discovered who the murderer is; it's time to turn him in.

Instead, I leaned on the fence and watched the horses. Four hours later, when Lonny came home, I was sitting in his living room in front of the fire I'd built, sipping chianti, more than half drunk.

Blue lay at my feet; I'd gone home to get him, thinking I'd call Jeri Ward from there. But my hand wouldn't reach for the phone, and when I'd climbed back into the truck I'd driven, as if on automatic pilot, back to Lonny's.

No amount of mental scolding seemed to break through my strange lassitude. I couldn't even fathom what I was feeling. Disbelief, pure and simple, washed over me like a wave and tumbled my emotions here and there whenever I thought of Bronc. How could he, I repeated over and over to myself, not knowing if I meant how could he kill Jack or how could he kill me.

Would he have killed me? I couldn't believe it. The very thought made the brilliant winter day look surreal, filled with ominous shadows and portents. When Lonny walked through his front door around four o'clock I was on my third glass of wine, telling myself, not for the first time, that it would fortify me for the call to Jeri.

Two hours after that, I lay next to Lonny in bed, in a strangely relaxed limbo. I'd told him my story; Lonny had been as shocked as I expected. Surprisingly, the situation seemed to breed in both of us a need for physical contact, and our comforting hugs soon escalated into full-blown lust. But even now, with lust behind us, for the moment, anyway, neither of us knew what to do about Bronc.

Lonny, the most conservative human being imaginable, had a hard time with the notion of turning Bronc in. And an even harder time contemplating the fact that he'd killed Jack. We simply clung to each other, wanting the reassurance of contact.

At long last I rolled my body away from Lonny's and said, "I'll go down to the sheriff's office tomorrow morning. That's good enough, don't you think?"

Pulling me back close to him, he murmured into my hair. "Whatever you think. And, yes, I think that's all right."

For a second I pressed myself as close as I could, feeling immeasurably grateful to have Lonny. Or to be had by him. Despite the day's turmoil my body felt soft and at long last my mind was relatively quiet. The contentment of good sex seemed to have tranquilized me.

"Even my toes feel good," I told him.

"Mmmm," he murmured sleepily. "Give me a few minutes and we'll try it again."

"More like an hour."

"So lie quiet and wait."

"And shut up?"

"That, too."

I did.

TWENTY-EIGHT

I never did have to turn Bronc in. The morning papers were full of the story. Bronc had written a note, confessing to Jack's murder, and left town taking his truck and trailer and Willy. Arriving at the ranch late that afternoon for another questioning session, Jeri Ward and Claude Holmquist had discovered the note and Bronc's escape.

Bronc never mentioned me. As far as I know, to this day Jeri Ward thinks I kept my word and stayed out of the investigation.

The Hollister Ranch remains in limbo. Having discovered the terms of Jack's will, the state is anxious to hold on to it, but Art Hoskins continues to press his claim and the whole thing is up to the courts to decide. Travis still lives there and takes care of it, for the time being. I hope things will fall Bronc's way and the ranch will become a park, but I wouldn't kill somebody to make it happen.

Bronc has, so far, simply disappeared off the face of the earth. The truck and trailer were recovered at a dealer's in the Central Valley, but there were no leads after that. Bronc had friends all over the state; I have to believe some team roper helped him out.

I sometimes wonder if I should have called the police immediately that day, made sure Bronc was arrested and paid the price for the life he took. Jack's life. I'm never convinced I made the right choice.

I wonder, too, if Bronc really would have killed me. If he'd held on to the rope. If Gunner hadn't outrun Willy. I'll never know, but I'll always believe not.

Bronc stays on my mind; I wonder if he rode to some lonely spot and killed Willy, then shot himself. It was something he might do. But sometimes I imagine him cowboying on a ranch in Nevada, riding Willy in the high desert, true to the end to his odd version of a Western code. I like to think of him finding a home at last, one far removed from the threats of developers.

It's a pretty idea.